I0762026

Demon Hunters

The Chronicles of Cassius

~ Volume One ~

Battle angel, demon hunter, guardian of lost souls,
meet Cassius, Heaven's holy avenger.

Yet disillusioned with his immortal existence,
he's one strike from falling.

Not all angels turn the other cheek.

The Children of Darkham
Titan Fall
Volgamare

Demon Hunters

Heroic Fantasy through the Ages

Books by Iestyn Long

The Timothy Williams Saga

Book One: Demon Hunter
Book Two: The Infernal Shadow

Demon Hunters

The Black Knight
Zen Lee & The Yellow Emperor
The Chronicles of Cassius

Demon Hunters

The Chronicles of Cassius

~ Volume One ~

Written by Iestyn Long

Illustrated by Trudy Harman

https://www.Demon-hunter.co.uk

ISBN: 978-1-9160177-7-1

Demon Hunters

The Chronicles of Cassius

~ The Children of Darkham ~

England, 1350

Ravaged by the Great Mortality, Lord Walter's estate of Darkham is plagued by a new horror. Someone or something is snatching children from their beds. The locals talk of strange things in the woods and a terrible wailing in the wind.

Cassius yearns for sunnier climes, but first, beneath the dismal grey skies of England, he must find Darkham's children and confront an ancient evil.

Demon Hunters

Heroic Fantasy through the Ages

Prologue

England—In the Year of our Lord, 1350

'Please, Lord, keep my children safe. Watch over them, protect them through this dark night.'

The storm raged, beating at the cold stone walls like howling banshees. The slatted wooden shutters barring the bed chamber's window groaned like the dead. Frightened, Mary Windle crossed herself. She knew there was more than wind and rain outside in the darkness.

Casting a final anxious glance at her sleeping children, Mary collected the stuttering lantern from the bedside table and walked from the room.

The Crusader

The solitary bell stopped ringing. Silence descended within the humble church of St Cuthbert. Mary Windle clasped her hands together and prayed to God. She pleaded for the safe return of Peter and Emma, begging the Almighty for his help. Already a week had passed since her beloved children were taken, ghosted away from their beds during that dark and terrible night.

It is my fault, she thought miserably. *If only we had abandoned this cursed place as I vowed.* Mary had lost her husband to disease, and now she had lost her children to evil. She had seldom felt such despair, but she was not alone.

Father Gilda spoke from the front of the church. 'Oh, Lord, in this time of desperate need, shine a light to guide us through the darkness. Wickedness plagues us. Help us cleanse it from our lands. Oh, Lord, we beseech you, send a heavenly host to drive the evil back whence it came, back to the infernal fires of Hell!'

As the monk's words faded, the church door swung open. Mary turned to see a man step into St Cuthbert's. For a fleeting moment, light penetrated the seething black storm clouds that gathered above the church, kissing him with its glory. Mary's breath caught in her throat. *He is beautiful. His hair gleams gold like the sun, and his eyes sparkle like sapphires.* Admittedly, Mary had not seen a sapphire, but what else could shine as brightly?

Who was this stranger? He was a knight; that much was certain. Mail and plate shone from beneath the man's flowing white robes, but she could see no sword sheathed at his side. *What knight does not carry a sword?*

Mary returned her attention to Father Gilda, who raged with condemnation from the altar. He blamed Darkham's plight on the French across the sea. Father Gilda liked to blame the French for every misfortune that he or his country suffered, great or small. After all, God was an Englishman, and all those who opposed England were nothing but the spawn of Satan.

Father Gilda fumed hysterically for what felt like an age. Mary suspected the monk was putting on a special show for Lord Walter's benefit. He and his entourage sat in the front row.

Darkham Hall was Lord Walter's estate. A tower on the hill, surrounded by a sprawling village. The estate had thrived until the coming of the Great Mortality, a remorseless and deadly plague. Two years had passed since the cruel pestilence swept the lands from south to north and east to west, putting half the population in the ground during its merciless journey, including Mary's husband, John. And now, a new horror haunted Darkham Hall.

'Thank you, Father Gilda,' Lord Walter said, raising his hands in praise. 'A service as good and wise as St Cuthbert's has ever known.'

Despite Lord Walter cutting short Father Gilda's ramblings, the monk beamed. 'I thank you, Lord. Kind words indeed.'

Lord Walter took Father Gilda's place at the front of the church. Lord Walter was a well-proportioned man except for a rounded paunch owed to many a full plate and tankard. He was a well-liked lord, at least as well-liked as any lord can be, fair and true with a good soul.

'As you know well enough, on the morrow is Christmas Day,' Lord Walter began, his mood sombre. 'Yet to spend this special time without so many of our beloved children is a heartbreak too far, especially when we have endured enough heartbreak to last a hundred years.'

The church echoed with mutterings of agreement. Darkham Hall, like every other settlement across the country, was ravaged by the Great Mortality. Not a single family in all of England had been left unscathed by the disease's deadly touch.

'And so, my friends, today I ride out side by side with my noble knights to put an end to the evil stalking our lands and to return our children to Darkham!'

Lord Walter's rousing oath stirred St Cuthberts into a frenzy.

'Praise be! Praise be!' Father Gilda cried, flinging his arms high and wide in joyous celebration.

Mary felt giddy with hope. At last, Lord Walter was committed to action. Somewhere out there were her children. They were hungry and frightened, but they lived. *I know they do. I can feel it.*

Following Father Gilda's service, Lord Walter and his knights gathered inside the church to discuss the particulars of their quest. Mary Windle and a good many villagers stayed to offer their support, and so did the white-robed stranger.

'We welcome your help, good sir knight, but perhaps it would not be freely given if you understood our task?' Lord

Walter had need of willing allies, but ever was he a fair man, and he would only accept this stranger's aid if the dangers of their quest were known to him.

'Fear not, Lord Walter,' the stranger replied. 'I know your purpose, and my offer stands. I am well versed in confronting the foul things of this world.'

An old man spoke from amongst the crowd. 'I tell you this, boy,' he rasped. 'You may have confronted many a foul thing in your time, but I'll wager none fouler than what I saw in them trees yonder.' The man, a wretched soul, pointed east with a wrinkled, shaking hand or at least where he thought east was. 'I saw creatures of the night, green-skinned and bowlegged, come from the wood. It was during the last full moon, the night as light as day, so I saw them good. Evil looking things they were, bent and twisted, and up to mischief.'

'It is true,' Sir Vilfort, Lord Walter's captain, said. 'We have sent men into the woods, but none have returned. Something sinister has taken root there.'

Father Gilda nodded profusely. 'Evil has cursed Greenwood, and all who enter fall prey to its malevolence!' the monk ranted fervently.

Compelled by a morbid curiosity, the stranger could not draw his gaze from the bulging veins throbbing at Father Gilda's temples. *If he rants with such vigour much longer, his head will surely implode.* The stranger took a wary step backwards. Should the worse happen, adequate distance between himself and the monk would be required if he were to avoid his white robes being splattered red. 'Good folk of Darkham, what else have you seen?' he asked.

'Such awful things, good sir,' began a sweaty wench, and by the circumference of her bloated belly, she was one pie shy of bursting. 'The children are taken from their very beds in the dead of night, but never a sound is made of their passing. No scream or cry of alarm. Ghosted away, they are. But folk have seen, good sir, seen things out in the dark, things born of the Devil!'

Trembling and writhing, Father Gilda's eyes rolled back into his head. It was as if a demonic spirit possessed him. 'The Devil!' he screamed, raising his shaking hands into the air. 'The Devil's work is upon us!'

The stranger did his best to ignore the monk's outburst. Quite frankly, it was embarrassing. Why so many of the Almighty's representatives on Earth were one turnip shy of a full vegetable cart was a mystery. 'I thank you for your honesty and warning,' the stranger said, 'but I remain steadfast.' He addressed Lord Walter directly. 'My sword is your sword, Lord Walter.'

Lord Walter grasped the stranger's hand. 'You have my eternal gratitude, sir.'

Confusion wrinkled the wench's greasy brow. 'But you haven't got a sword,' she said accusingly, observing the stranger's lack of weaponry.

'It is merely an expression,' the stranger explained. 'A verbal pledge in support of another. In this case, I offer my metaphorical sword to your lord for the duration of our expedition together.'

The wench looked none the wiser. 'Why haven't you got a sword?'

'I need no sword,' answered the stranger curtly. Inwardly, he wished the wench considerable misfortune. He reprimanded himself. *My behaviour is unbecoming of my position.* Yet containing his innermost feelings was forever a challenge, and year after year, his resolve to control such thoughts wore thin.

'What's he saying?' the old man croaked, cupping a withered hand to his one good ear. Determined to better see and hear this stranger, he squeezed his bony frame through the throng, but the effort proved too taxing, and he was required to rest his weary head between Sally Bishop's enormous daughters.

'He says he doesn't need one.'

'One what?' the old man crowed.

'He says he doesn't need a sword.'

'No sword? Pah! I'll wager he'll not come back from the cursed wood alive without one. A knight without a sword is like a badger without a snout.'

The stranger frowned. It was not the best analogy. *A wolf without his teeth might suit better.* Still, the man was old and infirm and barely in command of his bodily functions, and the comparison, however deluded, was commendable in the circumstances.

Sword or no sword, Mary Windle was cheered by the stranger's pledge. She did not know why, but he installed a burning hope within her soul. 'Are you a crusader, sir, like the noble knights of old?' she asked, mesmerised by his beauty.

Until now, with the exception of Lord Walter and 'fair-faced' Jane, the apothecary's wife, everyone she had ever met was either slack of jaw or pockmarked, and invariably both. *If this stranger is a crusader, should the red cross of his order not be visible upon his tunic?* Of which there was no sign.

The stranger decided he liked Mary Windle. At last, here was a peasant who could not only string a sentence together without sounding deranged but also showed him the respect he deserved. *I am too harsh on them,* he mused with a sigh. *They are but children. It is not their fault they lack the necessary intelligence. Their lives are too short to learn what must be known.* Nonetheless, remaining professional amongst the dim-witted whilst completing these tedious assignments was so very difficult.

Forcing his lips apart, the stranger smiled. 'My name is Cassius,' he said. 'And yes, I am a crusader of sorts.'

Morley

At noon, Lord Walter led Cassius and the knights of Darkham Hall from the village. Father Gilda blessed their departure, throwing handfuls of horse dung over the heroes for good fortune. Mary and the folk of Darkham praised the knights' courage and prayed for their souls. Yet more than anything else, they prayed for the safe return of their lost children.

A persistent icy rain falling from a grey, foreboding sky accompanied the ride through Lord Walter's estate. Soon Darkham was behind them, and atop their steeds, the knights journeyed toward distant Greenwood.

'Our strength is at a low, Sir Cassius,' Lord Walter explained on the way. 'If it is not the Great Mortality stealing our men, it is King Edward. He fights the French; he fights the Scottish; he fights the Welsh; he fights the Irish. If only he were here, I am sure he would fight the Devil. Alas, the burden is for us alone to bear.'

Cassius was familiar with King Edward's warmongering. 'England's sons and daughters pay a heavy price for their king's battle lust.'

Lord Walter sighed deeply. 'Aye, but the price must be paid.'

'Ever has it been so,' Cassius lamented. *The Devil whispers sweet promises into the ears of kings and queens, and in return, they feed the monster's depraved thirst with the souls of their dead.*

Before long, shrouded in the gloom, the leafless wood of their destination loomed. The trees appeared as dark shapes on the horizon, their naked branches like the twisted limbs of giants.

'Stout hearts, men,' Lord Walter called from the saddle. He knew the stories. Green-skinned men haunted these woods and other ungodly things besides. The villagers spoke of hearing shrill voices caught upon the wind and a terrifying wailing made by something neither man nor beast. *Whatever awaits us beneath the trees, we are ready*, Lord Walter told himself.

A barrage of fierce cawing met their arrival at the wood's edge. The knights cast their eyes to the high branches, where a host of nesting rooks shrieked with displeasure at their presence. If the ill omen was not bad enough, what followed was worthy of turning the stoutest hearts yellow, an episode to induce an uneasy quivering in the extremities of the rectum.

Beneath the skeletal branches of the winter boughs emerged a line of magnificent red stags. The animals pawed the wet leaf-strewn soil with cloven feet. Bellowing and snorting, they tossed their huge antlered heads, threatening to charge.

'The forest beasts are bewitched, my Lord. They guard our passage into Greenwood!' Sir Eustace declared. Unnerved, the knight felt the need to clench his buttocks and draw his blade for protection.

Never had Lord Walter witnessed such a display. 'A most peculiar sight,' he agreed. 'Yet I cannot believe these woodland creatures conspire against us.' Although not an expert in the ways of wild animals, he had hunted the beasts long enough to know they did not collaborate with one another nor arrange themselves into battle formations.

Cassius edged his steed alongside Lord Walter. 'Sir Eustace is right. This is the Devil's work administered by an acolyte of evil. Possession is a practice favoured by the forces of darkness. The witch or warlock responsible for this black magic hopes to discourage us from our task.'

Lord Walter appeared untroubled by the crusader's warning, dismissing the notion with a firm shake of his head. 'We shall advance at speed. I have yet to see a stag or woodland beast that does not flee when presented with a charging warhorse.'

Lord Walter knocked the faceguard of his helmet closed and pulled free his sword, just as Sir Eustace had done. 'Possessed or otherwise, let us chase these noble brutes back into the trees. At a gallop, men!'

The thudding of hooves pounded the soft earth and swiftly did the knights of Darkham thunder into the trees. The stags refused to relinquish their ground until the very last moment and well beyond what Lord Walter's men expected. The animals scattered all at once, quickly disappearing amongst the ash, elm, and oak.

The knights reined in their mounts at the fringes of the wood. 'A show of force to announce our purpose,' Lord Walter declared bullishly, pushing open his faceguard once more. 'If there is a witch, warlock, or some other wicked will at work within these woods, now they shall know of our intent, hey, Sir Cassius? We are not to be trifled with.'

'Indeed not, Lord Walter,' Cassius answered, and try as he might, he could not disguise the scorn from his voice. 'Any advantage gained from stealth is usurped by fearless valour. One and all shall now know of our presence and intent. A bold stance, my Lord.'

Lord Walter's bulbous nose twitched, and beneath his helmet, his brow wrinkled. 'Quite so, Sir Cassius,' he said, unsure how to take the crusader's words. 'We must call out the Devil's work where we find it, must we not?'

Cassius had not thought Lord Walter a fool. However, it seemed he was naive in matters of warfare, and in particular, warfare against the satanic denizens of Hell. Knowledge concerning the latter was to be excused. After all, not everyone was acquainted with the ways of demons and their masters. Yet as a lord of the realm, the former was his duty to know. If not for himself, then for the good of his people.

The men rode their nervous mounts deeper into the trees, persuading the skittish animals onwards with calls and clicks. The ground beneath the horses' hooves was soft and sodden, and the air cold and heavy, with low cloud causing a thick, misting precipitation.

Lord Walter gripped the reins of his steed tightly and the pommel of his longsword tighter. Despite his bold stance, he feared what might be found in the dark heart of this woodland. What manner of fiend stole children from their beds in the dead of night? Dreadful possibilities plagued his mind. Yet lingering on such unpleasantries served no purpose. Instead,

Lord Walter occupied his thoughts on the moment at hand and what needed to be done. Peering into the sombre grey mist, he searched between bough and branch for signs of evil in whatever ungodly guise it chose to wear.

Forging a meandering path beneath the trees, the knights continued onward. The rhythmic squelching and sucking of horses' hooves plodding through the rotted mulch and the persistent patter of rainwater against their helmeted heads became a dreary, monotonous beat. There was no sign of the antlered stags, the inhospitable rooks, nor any beasts native to the forests.

Cassius sensed evil. Like an invisible fog, the wood was shrouded in its cloying presence. It seeped into the dank soil, clung to rotted bark, and hung in the stagnant air. *The sickly-sweet smell of death,* Cassius mused grimly. It was everywhere, encircling them, waiting to feast upon their cold corpses.

'My Lord,' Sir Pottier's muffled voice drifted from the gloom. He was a skilled huntsman, and Lord Walter used the man's talents to help guide them through the woodland terrain. Suddenly, like a ghostly spectre, the knight materialised from the trees as if by magic. 'It seems we have stumbled upon a forgotten village.'

Ahead, the mature trees of Greenwood gave way to an area of much younger growth. Fragile saplings of ash and oak sprouted from the moist soil, and between them, a sprawling bed of weeds and thorns. Nature had taken little time reclaiming its lost lands from the people who once lived here.

A wave of melancholy darkened Lord Walter's soul. 'Morley,' he proclaimed sadly.

The knights trooped sombrely through the deserted village, their hearts heavy with the knowledge of what befell those who lived here. The thatched roofs of the timber cabins had decayed, and their walls had become choked with ivy. Some dwellings were nothing more than burnt-out husks, while others remained eerily well-preserved as if the occupants had vanished into thin air without warning.

Lord Walter halted within a meadow between the houses. In happier times, before becoming a burial site for Morley's dead, it was a communal green where villagers gathered to feast and dance. Now the clearing was overrun with vegetation. Creepers and nettles competed for dominance amidst thickets of bramble, and protruding between the undergrowth was a forlorn crop of wooden crosses.

'A sad sight,' Lord Walter remarked bleakly. 'Morley was once a prosperous place. Until the Great Mortality laid claim to all who lived here. It breaks my heart to see so many graves.'

Edging their mounts beside Lord Walter, the knights gathered to pay their respects, but Cassius was keen to move on. The air was rank with the stench of corruption. 'There is an unnatural presence here, my Lord. We should not linger.'

Nodding, Lord Walter conceded to the crusader's advice. 'Something tells me I should heed your council, good sir. I am convinced you can sense what we cannot. Come, let us leave this dismal place.'

Weaving their warhorses between the wooden crosses and beds of knotted weeds, the knights rode from the clearing to continue their quest. They passed what once was a church but was now nothing more than a blackened shell.

Cassius' gaze lingered on the sorry sight. *Churches ought to be built of stone. Timber is too easily consumed by the fires of Hell.*

Before returning to the shadows beneath the trees, Lord Walter wheeled his mount for a final farewell to Morley. 'Wait!' he ordered, raising a gauntleted hand into the air. 'Who among us remains behind?' he asked his knights.

Sir Vilfort manoeuvred his dappled grey charger until he faced the bleak scene once more. 'It is Sir Roger, Lord,' the knight answered, and like Lord Walter, he was confused by what he saw.

Head bowed, Sir Roger sat astride his steed, unmoving. It was as if winter ice had frozen him to his saddle. The knight's chestnut mare trembled in the rain, her nostrils flaring and wide eyes bulging with fright.

'Sir Roger,' Lord Walter called. 'What ails you, sir?'

The knight neither moved nor spoke.

Sir Vilfort guided his mount between the crosses again, rejoining his comrade at the centre of the graveyard. 'Come, Sir Roger, this is no time to contemplate the past.'

If Sir Roger heard Sir Vilfort's words, he made no sign. Seemingly oblivious to his surroundings, the knight remained subdued, his head slumped against his chest as if asleep atop his horse.

'Caution, Sir Vilfort,' Cassius warned. 'Something holds him against his will.' A swirling black mist only visible to Cassius rose from the cursed soil. *How inconvenient,* Cassius thought dryly. *The dead are rising.*

Sir Roger's head snapped upright, and from the depths of his helmet, his eyes blazed red like the burning coals within a blacksmith's forge.

'Feed us!' Sir Roger screamed, his voice childlike and desperate. 'Feed us with your blood!' The knight's hand twitched to the hilt of his longsword, and with a sudden jerk, he drew the blade into the chill, moist air.

'Sir Roger is possessed. The spirits have taken his soul!' Sir Vilfort cried, yanking his sword free from his scabbard.

Startled, Lord Walter's horse danced sideways, bucking and kicking. He clung to the beast's mane, yet the horse seemed sure to throw its rider. 'Steady, Sampson. Steady, boy!'

Swiftly, Cassius subdued the animal with soothing words. 'Calm yourself, horse,' he whispered, laying a steadying hand upon the beast's flank. 'Yes, good horse. We shall be gone from here soon enough.'

Lord Walter faced the crusader. 'We are at your mercy, sir. You alone among us have knowledge of such devilry. What must we do?' he pleaded, scared and panting hard like his mount.

Muffled by the dank winter rain, the clash of steel rang out through Morley. Sir Roger, a puppet for the dark spirit inside his body, slashed at Sir Vilfort atop his horse. 'Feed us. We must taste your flesh!'

Sir Vilfort turned Sir Roger's blade aside. 'He fights me as if I am his enemy!'

'Disengage, Sir Vilfort,' Cassius warned. If he did not, one knight would fall to the other regardless of past allegiances and friendships. The evil spirit cared for neither.

'I cannot. He is determined to slay me, sir.' Lord Walter's captain was doing all he could to prevent Sir Roger's longsword from slicing his head from his shoulders.

'Stand fast, Sir Vilfort,' Lord Walter encouraged. 'To arms, men!'

The knights of Darkham Hall dug their booted heels into the flanks of their steeds and sprung to Sir Vilfort's aid. Thundering into the graveyard, the knights surrounded Sir Roger, and from all sides, they pressed their mounts forward, squeezing him between them.

Denied space to wield his blade, the spirit compelled Sir Roger to scream with frustration. Promptly, Sir Richard knocked the weapon from the possessed knight's hands before Sir Mortimer and Sir Eustice hauled him from his saddle, dumping him into the dead leaves upon the cursed ground.

The things I must do for Heaven, Cassius moaned, sighing heavily. Leaping from his steed, the crusader straddled Sir Roger where he lay. Pinning the knight still, Cassius thrust the flat of his hand against the cold metal of his closed visor. 'Return from whence you came, child of Satan,' he commanded, hissing the words into the man's face. 'Begone!'

A blinding light pulsed from Cassius' palm, shining directly into Sir Roger's helmet. 'Go back to the pit. There is no place for you among the living. Go back to Hell!'

Fitting with rage, Sir Roger writhed beneath the crusader's grasp. 'No! Please, we beg you, we are hungry. We must feed!' He cursed, spat, screamed, defecated… and then, all of a sudden, he was still.

Cassius relaxed, and the light diminished. 'It is done.' Releasing his hold, he pushed himself from the knight's prone body. 'Quickly, return Sir Roger to his horse. We must be away from here. The dead are coming.'

Christmas Eve

Beneath the muddied hooves of the knights' horses, the earth shuddered.

'Morley has become a conduit between the living and the dead,' Cassius explained ominously, spelling out the grim truth of their blighted location. 'And unless we wish to share Sir Roger's ordeal or a worse fate, we must flee at once.'

Sir Rodger's memories of his terrifying episode were mercifully absent. However, the ordeal had affected him with a deep and disturbing sense of foreboding… and blindness to his eyes. 'I cannot see, damn it! I cannot see!'

Sir Cassius assured him that the condition was temporary, merely a consequence of exposure to holy light. And although blindness was not ideal in the circumstances—i.e., while hunting ungodly things within a haunted wood—full-on demonic possession would have proved considerably more demanding to live with.

The rumbling below them intensified, the foliage atop the graves shaking as the soil they were rooted within shifted. Wooden crosses began toppling, and a rising wind swirled around them, gusting like a cyclone.

Lord Walter required no further encouragement to vacate the area at speed. 'Withdraw!' he bellowed, and braving the unnatural gale raging through the clearing, he spurred his stallion into a gallop. 'To the woods and away!' he crowed. 'Away, I say!'

Sir Godfrey the Old—so named because he was old, although at what age he became known as Sir Godfrey the Old and not simply as Sir Godfrey is uncertain—and Sir Gilmore the Whistler—so named because of his mother's love of whistling, although why Sir Gilmore is the whistler, and not his mother, is anyone's guess—rode on either side of the afflicted Sir Roger, aiding the knight's retreat into the trees. Behind them, the wind howled, sounding as if the ghosts of the dead begged for their return.

Cassius waited for the others to flee before following. 'The ghosts of Morley cannot leave this place, not without a host, not without the living,' he called astride his black steed.

Deep inside Greenwood, far from Morley and its terrors, Lord Walter assembled his knights amidst a small glade. 'If the horrors of Morley are a taste of what is to come on this quest, then I pray for our souls. But to go back now…' He shook his head as if the notion were unthinkable. 'The guilt of our failure will darken our hearts until our dying day. And I, for one, could not live in such a way.'

'We have come this far, Lord. I say we finish what we started,' Sir Richard pledged. He was a loyal soldier, but by God, was he ugly. As a boy, he was disfigured by the pointed teeth of hungry wolves. The brave youth barely escaped the dreadful encounter with his life. In truth, many believed he should not have done, so ghastly was he to look upon. His appearance was enough to put the hardiest of souls off their breakfasts, not to mention their lunches and suppers. But not Lord Walter. While others forsook him, he took the boy under his wing and bid his master-at-arms train him as a knight.

Twenty years on, Lord Walter's kindness was being rewarded. 'I am with you, Lord.'

Regardless of Sir Richard's deformities, the knights of Darkham grunted their support for him and their lord. All except Sir Robin.

Sir Robin was no hero. 'Yet what of the demons, Lord? If Morley is evidence of what can be expected deeper into the wood, is it not folly to continue any further?' In fairness to the knight, his desire to be included in this quest was admirable, especially in light of his many fears. And thus far, to Sir Robin's credit, he had yet to soil his breeches—well, not as far as his comrades could tell.

'We have witnessed the Lord's grace at work, administered through the healing hands of his vessel, Sir Cassius, who I have reason to believe is not a knight at all but something more, something far greater.' Lord Walter's gaze found Cassius, and he smiled. 'Our guest is blessed by Heaven, my friends. At least, that is my hope. If that is indeed the truth of the matter, how can we turn back? He fights at our side, not by chance but by divine purpose. Spurning such heavenly aid would be a betrayal of God's trust, would it not?'

Cassius glazed over during the remainder of Lord Walter's rousing speech. He knew he ought not to have done, but rousing speeches were seldom anything but unimaginative. The same old thing time after time. Admittedly, and in defence of Lord Walter's efforts, Cassius had lived so long and witnessed so much that originality was hard to come by. Everything blurred into one. There were only so many words and ways in which to arrange them before the possibilities became exhausted.

Suddenly disheartened, Cassius peered up through the leafless branches at the leaden sky. *God, I miss the sun*, he mused longingly. Why was he not granted assignments in warmer, sunnier climes like in the good old days? He so missed vaporising mummies in Alexandria, slaying vampires in Venice, and hunting beautiful sand nymphs in Persia. He grinned devilishly. *How I loved hunting sand nymphs.* The nearest thing to a sand nymph here was a swamp hag. Cassius shuddered.

England was so wet and dreary, especially in the winter months. And the food was dreadful. How he yearned for a return to a Mediterranean diet. All they ate here was meat. Anything that moved was fair game. It was little wonder that so many of them suffered from gout. *Gout and flatulence*, he thought grimly.

Cassius had followed the Great Mortality's trail of devastation across Europe, combating the Dark Lord's demons who satisfied their malevolent appetites on the harvest of death and misery left in the disease's wake. Despite Cassius' incessant grumblings, he had a job to do—no matter where he was sent. Even if it was gloomy England where the Devil's work was rife.

Something lurked in Greenwood, an evil lingering amidst the oak and ash that he had not felt for an age. He could not explain what exactly. He searched his mind, delving through the endless memories hidden there… but to no avail. Whatever it was, it was waiting for him deep inside the forest.

The day wore on, and the skies darkened. A rumbling within the churning clouds promised fouler weather to come. Regardless of Cassius' dislike for the island's miserable climate, the cold rarely troubled him, at least not in the same way it did humans. Nonetheless, as the rain strengthened, tumbling from the iron-grey heavens with increasing ferocity, he pulled the cowl of his white robe over his head, covering the golden locks that fell in ringlets to his shoulders.

My new companions wear glum faces, Cassius mused, staring through the murk. *As I do.* The incident at Morley had left its mark on Lord Walter's knights, an open wound hounding their thoughts like a pack of rabid wolves. Left unchecked, the damage would fester until their minds were claimed by madness and despair. Cassius had seen it a thousand times before. Yet, haunted by evil as they were, their torment was countered by a desperate need to save Darkham's lost children. And by something more, by the presence of God—well, the presence of Cassius. In all honesty, he was a poor substitute for the Almighty. *Yet, as close as most mortals are likely to get to Heaven. Until their deaths, of course, and then only if they deserve it.*

'What a way to spend Christmas Eve, Sir Cassius?' Lord Walter remarked, slowing his mount to join the crusader at the company's rear. The horrors of Morley beset his thoughts, and he sought the companionship of others to distract his tortured mind.

'What a way indeed, my Lord,' Cassius replied wistfully. 'What a way indeed.'

Lord Walter studied the man riding beside him. The crusader was a mystery to him. His ageless face and how he spoke projected wisdom beyond his years. *An agent of the Lord sent to lighten our darkness?* It seemed implausible, but Lord Walter could not discount the man's heavenly qualities or actions. Expelling the hellish spirit from Sir Roger's body was evidence enough, was it not?

'You have a tale to tell; I see it in your eyes,' Lord Walter said.

Cassius sighed lamentably. 'If I enlighten you with my memories, my Lord, you will not believe a word I say.'

Lord Walter nodded sagely. 'Then keep them to yourself until you deem me wise enough to accept their truths.'

At once, Cassius' restless mind drifted into the distant past. He was there in Bethlehem on that fateful night, the first Christmas. Tasked with defending Heaven's newborn prince from the Devil's demons, he alone stood firm when all others fell. Cassius' heroics earned him great renown. He was favoured in those days. *My glory days*, he mused wistfully. *And now I hunt demons in the rain. As God wills it.*

Despite his lack of zeal for this assignment, the importance of his mission here in Greenwood was not taken lightly, and like that first Christmas, he would do everything in his power to save a child. *And Heaven willing, more than one*. Although, one would be better than none.

'It has been many a year since we have celebrated Yuletide as it ought to be celebrated. First, the Great Mortality, and now this cursed devilry has come between us and our faith. I wonder if we shall ever celebrate again,' Lord Walter continued miserably, his heart burdened with woe.

'You may, Lord Walter, and sooner than you think if Darkham's children are returned before the morrow.'

'What a Christmas that would be!' Lord Walter crowed, his face lightening with hope, but swiftly did his demeanour darken and his troubles return. 'Alas, I fear Greenwood shall be the death of me. If we must confront and vanquish an evil even half so twisted and deadly as the things haunting Morley, then I cannot imagine how victory can be gained.'

Contrary to his less-than-enthusiastic disposition, Cassius rested a compassionate hand on Lord Walter's armoured shoulder. 'Have faith, my Lord,' he said reassuringly. 'The darkest of shadows recede before the majesty of light.'

The knights of Darkham Hall lived on their nerves. Their helmeted heads jerked left and right at the merest disturbance, their unblinking eyes peering into the ever-thickening woodland.

'Lord, we must leave the mounts and continue on foot,' Sir Vilfort called from the vanguard of the small column. The path narrowed, and the way ahead was invaded by twisting moss-covered branches and tangling bramble.

'Agreed,' Lord Walter answered. 'What say you, Sir Cassius?'

Cassius gazed into the murk and between the boughs. This part of the forest was old, ancient even. 'It is sound advice, Lord Walter.' *The heart of Greenwood grows thick and strong.* 'Let us proceed on foot as Sir Vilfort suggests.'

The combined girth of both horse and rider could not hope to penetrate the density of the trees. And besides, there was little sense exposing the mounts as well as themselves to whatever horrors awaited them deeper in the woods.

'Fear not, horse, I will soon return,' Cassius whispered into the animal's twitching ear. He was fond of horses.

After tethering their beasts, the men gathered their weapons and shields, and then slowly and warily, they moved into the deepest, darkest part of the wood. Beneath the trees, it felt as if night had fallen early. The trunks and branches shielded much of the feeble winter light from the leaf-strewn soil below. It was disorientating to navigate the numberless boughs, and for what felt like an eternity, they wandered without truly knowing their direction. Yet as the day waned and the weather grew fouler still, the men of Darkham Hall smelt woodsmoke on the damp air, and through the trees, they saw a distant glow.

The Hollow

'Christ alive!' Cassius cursed. His robe had snagged on the barbs of a bramble bush, and as he had yanked the garment free from its clutches, its wicked spikes tore the hem. 'Damnable shrub!' A furtive glance into the trees confirmed Sir Walter and his knights suitably distanced not to have witnessed the angel's outburst. *Nor will they notice my subsequent act of retribution.*

Cassius channelled a brief but intense jet of holy light deep into the shrub's knotted heart. The offending branches swiftly blackened, shrivelling before the searing heat before crumbling to ash. *The cleansing fires of Heaven.* There was nothing quite like administering God's justice. The experience rarely failed to put a smile on his face. Great or small, nothing escaped the Almighty's righteous wrath, not even bramble bushes.

Cassius only hoped he had not inadvertently incinerated a family of moorhens or voles or whichever of Earth's insignificant creatures chose to nest in such a ridiculous location. He scolded himself, mentally at any rate. This was precisely the sort of behaviour that contributed to his fall from grace. In truth, if not for his extraordinarily-impressive demon-hunting skills, he would, in all probability, now be serving in Archangel Michael's army. Cannon fodder for the glorious Fifth Host. A short-lived position guaranteed to last no more than five minutes. *That or dispatched to the other side of the universe.* There was no shortage of heathen civilisations waiting to be subjugated and assimilated into God's 'club'. Implemented, of course, as peacefully as possible—unless the heathens became troublesome, in which case fire and brimstone were very much permitted.

Even though a change of scenery was tempting, it was not a career suited for the likes of Cassius. Long hours, scant rewards, and a strict dress code—i.e., you wear a dress—were examples of the many unpalatable working conditions. The position was beneath him. At least, Cassius thought it was. *I will not be going anywhere*, he thought grimly. Not every planet had demented fallen archangels caged within their cores. Earth was at the epicentre of all demon activity in the cosmos, thanks to the Devil and his unholy brethren. And no one was better at fighting demons than Cassius.

All life is sacred, Cassius told himself. Even the tiny furry creatures living in demonic bramble bushes. He sighed. *I want to be good, but it is such a chore.* Cassius was tired. Tired of spending countless years on Earth. Tired of hunting the Devil's own. Tired of pampering to the whims of mortals. He so wanted to retire. To spend the next millennia bathing in Heaven's light. *What a retirement that would be.* Yet only the worthy earned the right to perpetual rest at the Lord's side, and if Cassius desired such a reward, then he needed to be good… all the time.

Confident that his minor indiscretion had passed unobserved, Cassius made a conscious effort to focus. The sooner this assignment was concluded, the sooner he would be transferred elsewhere. Mind you, there were plenty of countries colder than England. *Please, I beg you, Lord, not Scotland.* Few places on Earth were less hospitable than the Isle of Mull on a cold winter's night. He counted himself fortunate that seldom was there a need to frequent icy landscapes. Demons detested the cold no less than angels, except trolls, ice giants, snow wraiths, frost wyrms, cave spiders, and the nasty Siberian devil tit. The little blood-sucking blighters were a nuisance everywhere north of Orkney. *And they take a particular liking to the extremities,* Cassius mused, remembering a previous somewhat painful assignment to the frozen lands of Norway. He still winced whenever he recalled his troll-hunting escapades with Gandalf, king of Alfheim, in the foothills above Ringerike. Still, the ale was recompense for any discomfort suffered at the vampiric birds' hands, or rather beaks. The trolls had been no problem. How he missed Gandalf and his extensive range of fruity yet obscenely potent ales.

And what will I find in the wild woods of England? The British Isles were a hotbed of devilry. In fact, nowhere else on the planet harboured such a host of demonic variants. Except for parts of Scandinavia… Oh, and Transylvania, where all sorts of hell lived—or unlived, to be accurate. 'It is the weather,' Cassius mumbled. 'Evil thrives in the shadows.'

As night loomed, Greenwood's darkening depths grew sinister still, if that were possible. Oak boughs became monsters' faces, ash branches the grasping hands of the undead, and the gusting wind shrieking between them the howling screams of lost souls. Drawn to the light, the knights crept through the winter wood, knowing their search for life amongst the barren trees and abandoned settlements was at an end. Yet what they would find at its source could only be guessed at, and none among them were naive enough to expect anything less than a living nightmare.

Abruptly, the tangled rows of oak and ash ended and beyond them was a treeless hollow. 'Let us approach with caution and with weapons drawn,' Lord Walter advised, peering from the trees.

At the foot of a shallow depression, several structures loomed bent and crooked in the gathering gloom. 'It is the old lumber mill,' Lord Walter whispered. 'The place was abandoned soon after the plague struck.' And now, the lumber mill and its cottage appeared reclaimed once more.

'Another boneyard,' Cassius observed bleakly. Wooden crosses littered the hollow's gentle slopes sticking from the ground at varying angles. It was a grim sight to match the gloomy weather.

'Just like Morley,' Sir Vilfort muttered. Fearing the spirits of the dead, Lord Walter's captain raised his longsword—not that a blade of steel or any metal would do the slightest bit of good against ghosts and wraiths, not unless the weapon was blessed, which, unfortunately, Sir Vilfort's was not.

Fanning across the oak-lined ridge, Lord Walter and his knights started down the slope, weaving between the graves with their sad crosses of remembrance. Now exposed under the open skies, the rain hammered against them unhindered, swept sideways across the woodland glade by shrieking gales. With their cloaks whipping in the wind, the knights descended toward the brooding timber buildings, each step a battle against the rising storm.

Sorcery is at work. The elements are bent to another's will, Cassius mused ominously. He hoped a warlock was not to blame.

Warlocks were lords of the dark arts and the most powerful of the Devil's acolytes. Summoning, necromancy, elemental control, shape-shifting, possession, suggestion, and every other form of black magic known to man, warlocks were masters of them all. Every evil king or queen worth their salt had at least one to do their bidding. By 1199AD, King John of England had recruited seven to his wicked cause, one for every day of the week.

Britain was ever rife with warlocks, Cassius thought. *Let us pray their kind has not returned to prominence.* Be that as it may, he liked vanquishing warlocks almost as much as he did goblins. Cassius despised goblins. *The Devil's minions. Treacherous miscreants of filth. Damn them all.* Mind you, warlocks were a lot harder to kill.

Nearing the structures, Lord Walter angled his approach toward the ramshackle cottage. Of the two buildings, the house was occupied without question. A warm glow issued from behind shuttered windows, and a swirling smog rose from a lopsided chimney before being carried away by the strengthening winds.

Lord Walter fixed his eyes on the weather-worn door ahead. He did not dare drop his gaze for fear of missing whatever lurked within evade his observations. Distraction, if only for a moment, could mean his death. *I must remain vigilant.* Beneath his breastplate, his heart pounded. Although glistening with icy rain, his mouth was as dry as dust and his breath as hot as fire. The soil beneath Lord Walter's feet was fast becoming a treacherous sludge, and more than once, he lost his footing amidst the mire. Yet despite each misplaced step, Lord Walter's unwavering gaze remained firmly glued upon the cottage and its weathered door.

The rain eased, the winds calmed, and quite unexpectedly, the storm battering Greenwood ceased. In its place, an eerie stillness settled over the hollow, as unnatural as it was unnerving.

'Be on your guard, Lord Walter,' Cassius warned. 'Dark magic is at hand.' Like a poisonous fog, he felt its presence. It clouded his thoughts, burned his lungs, and crawled beneath his skin. The source of this devilry oozed from within the cottage. 'It would be wise if I went on ahead.'

Lord Walter dearly wished to accept the crusader's request, but he and he alone was responsible for what was happening here. Darkham was Lord Walter's estate, and he was answerable to its people. Before risking the lives of his men, he would first risk his own. 'No, sir, the honour is mine.'

There is no honour in dying, Cassius thought dryly. Be that as it may, he understood the man's reasons, even if they were foolhardy.

In front of Lord Walter's unblinking eyes, the cottage door gradually groaned open. Swallowing hard, he took a deep breath and prepared himself for the monstrosity he was set to face. Silhouetted by firelight, a figure stood beneath the arch of the door. Dropping his shield into the mud, Lord Walter knocked open the steel visor covering his face. 'Eleanor?' A shuddering jolt of elation flooded Lord Walter's body, tempered almost immediately by shock and confusion. 'Is it truly you?'

Cassius glanced to Sir Vilfort for answers.

'Lady Eleanor is Lord Walter's wife,' Sir Vilfort explained, appearing no less perplexed than his lord. 'I speak false, Sir Cassius,' he conceded grimly, his voice barely above a whisper. 'Lady Eleanor was Lord Walter's wife. She has been gone these past two years, succumbing to the Great Mortality along with Lord Walter's daughter, Agnes. Yet here they both stand, risen from their graves. What cruel sorcery is this?'

A second woman now stood with the first. Slipping and sliding through the mud, Lord Walter hastened toward them.

'No, Lord Walter!' Cassius cried. 'They are not your wife and daughter!'

The crusader's warning checked Lord Walter's advance, his words like shards of light piercing the shadow cloaking his thoughts. *Something is wrong. How can my loved ones be here?* Had he not watched his faithful Eleanor and then his darling Agnes fade away before his very eyes? Had he not stared aghast as their caskets were lowered into the earth?

'Husband, come to us,' Lady Eleanor called, beckoning Lord Walter to her.

'Yes, Father, come to us.'

Lord Walter was torn between believing the stark reality of what stood before him and the truth of the memories swirling inside his mind. In flesh and blood, here was his family, but he remembered they no longer lived. Lord Walter raised his sword. 'What are you?'

The women laughed, cruel and mocking. Yet swiftly did their laughter become cries of anguish. Mother and daughter wailed in misery, their bodies withering and putrefying. Lord Walter could do nothing but stare in horror as his family rotted before his disbelieving eyes. Maggots oozed from their rancid skin, teeth blackened, eyes bulged, bowels loosened… and forthwith, a bout of flatulence both fetid and foul ripped through the dank clearing like nothing the good knights of Darkham Hall had witnessed before.

An unholy stench laid the knights low, and as they retched their guts up through their throats, gagging and spitting on their bitter bile, the doors of the old lumber mill exploded outwards, and bursting through the splintered timbers sprang a monstrous thing of nightmare.

The Hell Beast

'Oh, joy,' Cassius despaired. 'A red skin.' The evening, he decided, was rapidly becoming a chore.

At ten feet tall with blistered crimson skin, claws like scimitars, and a face so hideous that not even its own mother could stomach the sight of without vomiting—if indeed the creature had a mother, which Cassius seriously doubted—a red skin was a fearsome proposition. *I would rather face a warlock.* Nonetheless, the demon's presence raised questions. What was it doing here? And who had summoned it?

Residing deep within the fiery pits of Hell, the demons were not known for taking vacations to the cold, wet English countryside. Nor did they have the means to organise such a trip if they so wished, at least not without the aid of some particularly potent dark magic. The power required to summon creatures from Hell is considerable. Cassius doubted that even King John's warlocks had managed the feat. However, he did recall the Sheriff of Nottingham raising an army of the dead to overthrow England's barons. Although not as impressive as summoning pit dwellers, it was nonetheless a notable demonstration of the dark arts.

Unless there is a portal hereabouts? Cassius mused. *Which would be just my luck.*

It was rare, thank the Lord, but now and then, Lucifer conspired with his demon underlings to create gateways to the world above. Over the centuries, the practice had become a game of cat and mouse between Heaven and Hell. Lucifer would open a portal and send forth his demons. In answer, Heaven dispatched its angels, but by the time they arrived on the scene, the demons had invariably dragged their victims kicking and screaming into Hell. To save face, the angels would obliterate the portal before repeating the process the following Tuesday or whenever the Lord of Shadows next felt bored.

Over the centuries, Cassius had been tasked with locating and destroying many of these gateways, but he dismissed the thought, questioning the Devil's interest in Darkham. *What would the Fallen One want with such an insignificant backwater?* No, whoever was behind this foulness was acting on their own behalf. *Yet they are powerful indeed to summon red skins.* And not forgetting the reanimation of the dead in such meticulous detail as to persuade the living of their authenticity. Lord Walter had been convinced of his wife and daughter's existence. Yet the uneasy feeling nagging Cassius' thoughts would not fade. He could not help but think there was something else at play here, something he could not put his finger on.

Sir Reginald the Unflustered, freshly returned to Darkham Hall from his exploits in France fighting for good King Edward, stared in mortification at the terrible thing racing toward him. He had never seen the like of this dreadful foe before, not across the sea in the green fields of France, not in the sprawling forests of England, not in the hidden valleys of Wales, and not in the rugged mountains of Scotland where everyone and their mothers were demons—or so Sir Godfrey the Old claimed.

As the abomination drew near, splashing through the filth beneath its taloned feet in huge bounding strides, Sir Reginald noted its ungodly features: slavering maw, uncommonly large teeth, and huge red eyes that blazed in the falling darkness like glowing brands.

Sir Reginald found himself becoming increasingly flustered.

'Run!' Cassius cried. But the knight was rigid with fear, and as the crusader sped to his aid, cursing under his breath about the ineptitude of humans en route, Sir Reginald was disarmed… literally. *Oh, dear,* thought Cassius wincing.

After a single deadly swipe, the beast's razor-sharp claws had ripped the knight's sword arm, including sword, from his body. Frozen with terror, Sir Reginald appeared not to have noticed the sudden loss of his favoured limb. Only after bright-red blood began spurting intermittently from the stump did he realise that something was amiss, and by then, of course, it was too late.

'Withdraw, Sir Reginald!' Lord Walter bellowed, tearing his eyes at last from the festering corpses crumpled at his feet, corpses that had once resembled his wife and daughter. Yet even as his words issued from his lips, Sir Reginald's severed head joined the skeletal remains of Lord Walter's loved ones upon the sodden ground.

'Forward as one!' Lord Walter ordered. He had seen enough to realise this monster was more than a match for any of them. *Yet together, there is a chance to send this monstrosity back to Hell.* Swearing an oath on the lives of the dead, he vowed to see the demon fall or die in the attempt.

'You heard Lord Walter!' Sir Vilfort yelled, seeing the men falter, fear leeching the courage from their hearts. 'We attack as one!'

Trudging through the mud, Lord Walter joined Sir Mortimer, Sir Eustace, Sir Robin, and Sir Godfrey the Old—whose sword arm trembled as frequently as Sir Mortimer's bottom lip, which was nearly as much as Sir Robin's bottom. From the opposite side of the hollow approached Sir Vilfort, Sir Pottier, Sir Roger, Sir Richard, and Sir Gilmore the Whistler—who presented with certain death at the hands of a terrifying ten-foot-tall demon had discovered to his surprise, that he could whistle like his mother after all, albeit not from the expected orifice.

As dusk deepened and the light diminished, the storm returned just as suddenly as it had stopped. Howling winds drove a horizontal deluge stinging across the woodland glade, and now, with its claws slick with Sir Reginald's blood and its tortured crimson skin sizzling and steaming in the rain, the monster roared a defiant challenge to the advancing knights.

Fighting a crippling sense of dread, Lord Walter dragged himself onward into the storm, inching ever closer through the mud toward his frightful opponent. Yet then, as he and his knights prepared to meet the beast in battle, the voice of an angel sang through the hollow for all to hear.

'Out of my way!' Cassius demanded, barging past Lord Walter like a bull charging after a red rag. 'This foe is beyond any of you. I alone must face the beast!' To be honest, Cassius was far from enthralled at having to engage the demon in mortal combat. He was cold, and it was raining.

On the other hand, failing to intervene would almost certainly result in the swift and gruesome demise of Lord Walter and his knights. And Cassius had no desire to spend the remainder of his already ruined evening fishing their dismembered body parts from muddy puddles. However, despite his reluctance, it was his sworn duty as a holy angel to defend the helpless. If Cassius was ever going to retire to Heaven, he needed to start completing his assignments without all the humans getting killed in the process.

'How will you fight without a sword?' Lord Walter bellowed into the wind.

It was a fair point well made. How would Cassius fight and vanquish a hell beast without a three-foot length of sharpened steel at his disposal?

The seraphim, guardians of Heaven, wielded swords of fire. In certain circumstances, when the situation at hand required something with a bit more oomph, these all-powerful weapons were loaned to the archangels and, even though it was rare, to angels like Cassius. In times past, he had been fortunate enough to brandish such a blade.

Alas, this was not one of those times.

How I would dearly love to wield a sword of fire again. Cassius cast the fanciful notion from his thoughts. The chances of the seraphim entrusting him with another of their sacred blades were highly improbable, especially after what had happened the last time they had done so, an episode Cassius vehemently denied responsibility for even to this day. *It matters not,* he thought, striding at the hell beast. *A sword of my own making will suffice.*

Gleaming in the growing darkness, a blade materialised within Cassius's right hand, forged entirely from angel light. Manipulating divine energy was a skill mastered by but few. Cassius' repertoire included swords, spears, tridents, and shields. He could also twist angel light into the shapes of animals. Children loved them at birthday parties, at least until the creations escaped and burned down their parents' homes.

'He does have a sword!' Lord Walter declared, his voice quivering with wonderment.

Cajoled from monotony by his audience's rapture, Cassius felt compelled to put on a show. He knew vanity was not the best trait for an angel to possess, but it was impossible to ignore. And besides, where was the harm in enjoying a little attention now and then, especially when he was risking his neck for the sake of others?

With a surging flash, Cassius blazed with light. His white robes, silver armour, and every inch of his body shone like the stars in the night sky.

Lord Walter and his knights bowed their heads in reverence, shielding their eyes from the harsh glare. 'By all things holy,' Lord Walter cried. 'What are you, sir?'

Cassius stood amidst the gloom radiating like the sun. 'I am a servant of Heaven, tasked with casting demons into Hell,' he proclaimed. 'Which, I might add, is a role I perform exceedingly well.' Cassius shuddered with pleasure. Oh, how he adored the attention.

The snarling red skin leapt high into the turbulent skies. Descending through the rain, the demon crashed into the angel, determined to smash him into oblivion. Sinking to his knees, Cassius threw a shield of light between himself and his enemy. The creature slammed against the barrier, its claws raking the shimmering surface, desperate to maul the angel beneath.

Under the hell beast's weight, Cassius was pushed deep into the mud. As he sunk lower and lower—the squelching sludge quickly rising past his chest—he dispatched a shaft of light from his sword. The holy blast punched the pit dweller howling into the filthy night, and like a steaming red missile, the creature flew through the rain until it crash-landed into the hollow's slopes.

Lord Walter had harboured hope that the crusader was Heaven-sent, and now that hope was realised. If the Almighty was fighting for them, how could they fail?

'In our time of need, Heaven sends us an angel!' Sir Godfrey the Old proclaimed, and his sword arm no longer trembled like a leaf in the breeze. Instead, he held his weapon with renewed strength and an unfailing iron-like grip.

'God bless you, sir!' Sir Robin gushed, and like Sir Godfrey, he had rediscovered his courage and the ability to control his quivering bottom.

Hauling himself from the mud, Cassius cringed. There was only so much adoration he could stomach before feeling nauseous.

Buried deep within the hollow's southern slope, the red skin worked feverishly to dig itself free. Excavating huge handfuls of moist soil from its path, it erupted from the oozing, slack bank, mud-splattered and hissing in the rain. Roaring to the hidden moon, the monster's red eyes glowered at Cassius from across the clearing.

'Oh, wonderful,' Cassius moaned. 'Now I have made the thing angry.'

Lurching forward, the red skin ploughed through the mire, trampling the wooden crosses beneath its feet, desecrating the graves of the dead.

'Lord Walter, while I entertain the beast, might I suggest you and your men search for the children?'

The angel's request was so calmly conveyed that, at first, Lord Walter failed to recognise the urgency of the situation. To be honest, Lord Walter might have been forgiven for thinking Sir Cassius was inviting him to attend a Bible reading at Saint Cuthberts or an all-you-can-eat banquet at his hall and not to search in all haste a cursed lumber mill for warlocks and lost children. As it was, Lord Walter stood amidst the driving rain like a statue, oblivious to the angel's polite demands, no matter their relevance or importance.

The storm hammered the two adversaries, but to Lord Walter's staring eyes, the raging weather affected neither. The rain vaporised on contact with the demon's fiery hide, shrouding the pit dweller in a cloud of rising steam. And while the howling wind bent the trees ringing the hollow back and forth, the angel below appeared unruffled, and not a single ringlet cascading from his golden head was displaced.

The angel began glowing brighter as he prepared to accommodate the red skin's charge. 'Lord Walter? If you would be so kind as to begin your search?' Cassius repeated, demonstrating the patience of a saint. Although, beneath the surface, he was, of course, screaming profanities at the man's lack of urgency.

'Oh, yes. Of course, Sir Cassius. Forgive me,' Lord Walter blurted, finally coming to his senses. 'Sir Vilfort, take half the men into the mill. The rest of you follow me.' The angel was right; this foe was beyond them. It was far better to leave the Devil's minion to God's acolyte and for the rest of them to find the children while they had the chance.

Stumbling away into the night, Lord Walter headed toward the cottage and Sir Vilfort, the lumber mill. Behind them, glowing red and gold amidst the heart of the storm, Heaven and Hell went to war.

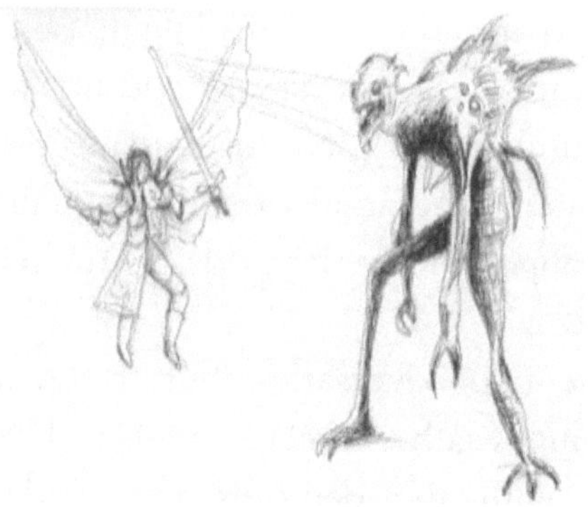

The angel's sword blazed in the darkness, arc after slashing arc of dazzling white light flashing through the rain. As each blow landed, showers of dancing sparks exploded into the cold, moist air, and like swarms of fireflies, they were swept upwards into the night and borne away on the winds to be scattered amongst the bare branches of Greenwood.

Yet the hell-beast prevailed.

'For God's sake, hurry up and die, damn you!' Cassius cursed with frustration. Having lost his audience, the thought of continuing the contest to its bitter end was less appealing, especially in light of his opponent's reluctance to drop dead.

Red skins are ever troublesome to put down, Cassius reminded himself. Each slash of his sword of light was repelled by the thing's fire-toughened hide. *Hide,* he mused irritably, *enhanced with enough black magic to birth a second Dark Age.* And with his hands tied fighting the demon, Cassius feared Lord Walter and his knights would be at the mercy of the red skin's master.

The Witch

At the lumber mill's broken gates, Sir Vilfort paused. It was as black as pitch inside. The dark was briefly dispelled by shards of red and gold flashing from the combatants duelling in the night.

'Something resides within,' Sir Richard whispered. He could not see anything moving amid the blackness, not even when the light flickering from the hollow lit the mill, but he sensed a presence, an almost tangible malevolence curdling the dank air.

'Is it the children, do you think?' Sir Pottier questioned, more in hope than expectation.

'Perhaps,' Sir Vilfort replied, 'or else some other ungodly thing waiting for us in the shadows.' He stared anxiously into the gloom. What *was* lurking within?

Behind them, the red skin's piercing howls tore into the night sky, a chilling accompaniment to the relentless wailings of the storm. 'Come,' Sir Vilfort said, 'Sir Cassius does his duty, now must we.'

Huddled close, the men of Darkham edged warily through the darkness. They could see little, less even than Sir Roger post-demonic possession. The wind shrieked through gaps in the building's timber frame, and high in the rafters, a shutter banged in the wind over and over. *A drum roll to the gallows*, Sir Vilfort thought miserably. *Do we march to our doom?* He fought to control his breathing, which had begun to quicken like the beating heart of a startled fawn. Deeper into the mill, a stomach-churning aroma hung in the chill air, thick and pungent that caught in the throat.

'The air grows foul,' Sir Richard declared, gagging. 'What is that ungodly stench?'

'Something left to rot,' Sir Pottier answered, desperately trying to quell his heaving guts. Revisiting one's breakfast inside one's helmet was not a pleasant experience, and the scent of stale vomit was hell to shift.

Half-blind, they stumbled on, wading through oceans of sawdust and clambering over heaped mounds of split logs and piles of moss-covered timber abandoned to decay.

'I cannot see a damn thing!' Sir Gilmore growled.

An instant later and the knight's lack of perception was confirmed. A metallic clang reverberated through the darkness as Sir Gilmore's helmeted head slammed against a low beam. His brothers-in-arms winced, not out of sympathy for Sir Gilmore's battered forehead nor his bruised ego but for almost certainly alerting whatever lurked within to their presence.

Things were moving out there in the blackness. Sir Pottier could hear the scratching and scurrying of clawed feet… and perhaps the gnawing of teeth? 'Rats,' he hissed. *But what do they gnaw?* Images of festering corpses crawling with ravenous vermin flashed before his eyes. Sir Pottier grimaced. *My thoughts are as grim as the grave.*

'Children, are you here?' Sir Vilfort yelled into the gloom. The time for skulking in the shadows was over. Sir Gilmore's untimely union with a gnarled length of wood had curtailed the element of surprise.

Deep inside the mill, muffled murmurings, seemingly in response to the captain's call, drifted like ghostly echoes to their pricked ears.

'Did you hear?' Sir Richard whispered. 'There *is* something alive in here apart from cursed rats.'

With no thought given to what might be lingering in the shadows, the knights blundered through the shrouded confines of the lumber mill, hoping beyond hope to find Darkham's children waiting for them. Blinded by darkness, they sped headlong into the structure's sprawling night-black depths. Feeling their way through the gloom, they stumbled into a larger chamber, and here they skidded to a halt, their eager charge at an end. Gleaming in the blackness like a swarm of demonic fireflies floated scores of devilish red eyes.

*

Holding his sword and shield with shaking hands, Lord Walter crept warily inside. The smell of stewed meat and vegetables greeted him, rich and enticing. 'Rabbit?' he mumbled in confusion.

A pot bubbled over a crackling fire, and a table was set for supper beside the stove. Vases and jars of varying sizes lined the shelves, but they were not stuffed with the eye of newt, the wing of bat, or the spleen of weasel, yet with roots, herbs, and seasonings. Game and not severed heads hung from the rafters. Tomes and not bones filled the spaces. *Where are the implements of torture or whatever disciples of evil secrete in their nooks and crannies?*

This was a scene of modest homely comforts and not the lair of devilry Lord Walter was expecting. Yet then, tucked away in a shadowy corner of the cottage, he saw her—and how he had not done so sooner was a mystery. Fondling a purring black cat nestled contentedly between her thighs, a grey-haired woman rocked back and forth in a creaking armchair. She sat gazing through a small open window. Despite the storm's ferocity, neither the rain nor wind encroach within.

'Margery?' Fresh horror coursed through Lord Walter's veins. Was this another abominable apparition like Eleanor and Agnes? Would he be condemned to witness his sister and her beloved cat, Mittens, rot before his eyes just as he had done his wife and daughter? Nonetheless, it was the sinister figure watching from Lady Margery's side that caused his heart to quicken. A green man.

Man, however, was not an accurate description. Ugly as sin and misshapen beyond reason, the wart-ridden creature leered with beady pig-like eyes that gleamed red in the firelight. The thing did not so much stand as it did lurch. Lord Walter noted how its unnaturally long fingers, which ended in horrible black claws, tightened around the haft of a brutal-looking axe. *The creature seems eager to bury that weapon in my skull.*

'Greetings, Brother,' Lady Margery spoke, refusing to avert her attention from the battle raging outside. 'Your angel fights well.' Blinding light flared spasmodically, flashing through the window, appearing more vivid now darkness had fallen.

Lord Walter reeled as if struck because now he understood the dreadful truth. 'I beg you, Margery, tell me this is not your doing?' Although, as awful as it was to believe, he already knew the answer. *I pray it is not so.*

'It is,' she stated nonchalantly, continuing to caress her cat with long affectionate strokes.

'Why, Sister?' Lord Walter implored, sickened to the stomach by what his flesh and blood had become. And what had she become? *A witch,* he thought grimly. *Regardless of the false façade she projects.* Appearances could be deceptive, and there was no greater deceiver than evil. The children's trust in a familiar face would have made their abduction all too easy. Before her disappearance, Lady Margery was a teacher in Lord Walter's hall, educating Darkham's children. *The same children she has betrayed.*

'Who am I to refuse Beelzebub's calling?' Lady Margery hissed fiercely.

Lord Walter grimaced. If he were not carrying a sword and shield, he would have crossed himself—and more than once. 'This is witchcraft and devilry! You dabble in things you do not understand.'

Finally, lifting her gaze from the window, Lady Margery met her brother's troubled eyes. 'Oh, but I do,' she whispered. 'My master's rewards are plentiful. The children are but a small sacrifice in exchange for power. Soon I will drain them all and wield a force beyond reckoning!'

His sister's zeal shocked Lord Walter, and he stumbled backwards, fearing for his life. Finding his courage once more, he pointed his longsword toward the disgusting, *green man* poised at her side. 'And pray tell, what is this hideous wretch?'

The creature growled menacingly.

'A handsome fellow, do you not agree? He and his kin aid my work here and—' Lady Margery's words fell silent, but in their stead, she emitted a heart-stopping scream. Jerking her head sideways, she returned her gaze to the hollow.

While Lady Margery was distracted, Lord Walter seized his chance to escape her unwelcome company. Spinning, he bundled himself from the cottage, upturning the table and knocking the stew into the fire in his haste. Outside amidst the storm, he understood his sister's anguish.

Entwined in combat, Sir Cassius and the red skin were encompassed within a sphere of shining light. It shone so brightly that Lord Walter and his knights were forced to avert their gaze lest their eyes melt like candlewax before flame. For a time, the hollow was lit in perfect clarity, as if the morning sun shone above them. The angel held his searing sword two-handed, the holy weapon's glowing length firmly skewered through the beast's writhing torso.

Lord Walter praised Sir Cassius' courage. Earlier, the angel appeared unaffected by the elements lashing from the black skies and impervious to the monster's terrible wrath. But now, he was beaten, bruised, and battle-worn. Soaked to his bones, his golden curls were plastered across his battered face, his armour scarred and dented by raking claws, and his white robes shredded and cast into the mud. It was plain to see the angel's victory had been hard-fought and hard-earned.

Gritting his teeth, Cassius wrenched his blade free from the red skin's chest. Immediately, the monster's howling ceased, and the heat pulsing from its fiery hide cooled, hardening until the demon was transformed into a blackened husk.

'It is over,' Cassius announced wearily. Now nothing more than a ghastly statue, the hell beast remained upright, frozen in death, its arms stretched wide and its contorted face angled toward the heavens. In a final act of rage, the angel swept his sword of light down upon the demon, instantly vaporising the creature's crusted shell into dust.

While the monster's remains dispersed far and wide on the winds, Cassius' gleaming blade faded. The battle was ended, but a debilitating lethargy consumed the angel. 'It appears… that I have… overextended myself,' he muttered feebly. 'I think… I will rest awhile. My apologies for the… inconvenience.' Overcome with exhaustion, Cassius slumped face-first into the mire. The glowing sphere surrounding him vanished, leaving the hollow cloaked in darkness.

'Sir Cassius?' Lord Walter said, shaking him, but he could do nothing to rouse the angel from his slumber.

'What has befallen him?'

'The demon has struck our friend a grievous blow, Sir Mortimer,' Lord Walter replied. 'Help me manoeuvre him so his lungs do not fill with mud.' Between them, the knights rolled the angel onto his back. Whatever injury afflicted him, it seemed there was little that could be done. 'We must prove ourselves worthy without the angel's help.'

Now that the storm-torn night had reclaimed the hollow, plunging everything into blackness once more, Lord Walter's beleaguered eyes were drawn to the light spilling from the cottage. In contrast to the vibrant glare commanded by Sir Cassius, a soft orange hue glimmered through the open door. Silhouetted within that light stood Lady Margery, cat lovingly cradled in the crook of her left arm and in the other a curious staff tipped with a glittering crystal. 'Do you know how many lives it cost to summon him?' she shrieked into the storm, her face bent with rage.

The feline's pointed bat-like ears flattened in alarm. Lord Walter saw how the creature's eyes shone red like those of the grotesque green man who waited with axe in hand, looming behind his sister like a baleful shadow.

'Because of the ill-advised actions of your foolish angel, more children must die.' Lady Margery sneered at Lord Walter's knights as they edged nearer with swords raised. 'What hope do you have without your heavenly protector?' The woman's twisted features shifted toward Lord Walter. 'I am dearly sorry, Brother, but to bring forth my demons, I must have *all* your lives.'

'Where are the children, Margery?' Lord Walter demanded. She was his responsibility, and she would meet justice. 'Tell me, and your death will be swift, I swear. Fail to do so, and it will be the fire for you.'

Lady Margery sniggered contemptuously and whispered into her cat's twitching ears. 'Did you hear that, Mittens? We are to be cast into the flames. What do you think about that?'

Raising its hackles, the black feline's red eyes glowered. 'The knights of Darkham will die!' the creature hissed, its voice unexpectedly deep and menacing.

All at once, Lord Walter's men soiled themselves. 'May the Lord give us strength!' Godfrey the Old cried, his hands trembling like never before. Lady Margery was beyond salvation, and so was her despicable familiar.

'Sister, I offer you one last chance. Surrender yourself and renounce the Devil or face the consequences!'

'Never!' Lady Margery screamed. She hawked and spat into her brother's open visor, then flung Mittens straight at his face.

Using the flat of his sword, Lord Walter batted the cat aside, but in doing so, he inadvertently diverted the animal toward Sir Roger. The feline thumped against the knight's upraised shield, digging its claws into the surface. Panic-stricken, Sir Roger stumbled backwards before collapsing into the mud.

Determined to tear out the knight's throat, the demonic cat scrambled the length of Sir Roger's shield before scratching feverishly with its claws, seeking a gap in his armour.

'Hold still, Sir Roger,' Sir Godfrey the Old yelled, battling to steady his shaking hands. He loomed above the fallen knight, poised to strike.

'Are you sure, Sir Godfrey? Your eyes are not what they once were!' Sir Roger knew only too well how a lack of vision hindered the simplest tasks: ducking tree branches, urinating without getting wet boots, knowing which way to point your sword when confronting the enemy…

Thankfully, Sir Roger's blindness had been short-lived. Although, and not for the first time since his sight had been restored, seeing Sir Godfrey's blade plunge toward him, he half-wished it had not. He would almost rather risk the cat's slashing claws than Sir Godfrey's sword... almost. Unable to watch, Sir Roger clamped his eyes shut and beseeched the Almighty to guide the old knight's blade.

A squelching thud against Sir Roger's shield curtailed a high-pitched screech.

'Well done, Sir Godfrey!' Sir Roger praised, daring to open his eyes once more. 'I did not doubt you for a moment,' he lied, gingerly scrapping the two halves of dead cat from his bloodied shield.

The loss of Mittens was a terrible blow to Lady Margery's morale. Great wailing sobs exploded from deep within her cursed body. Overcome by grief, her command of the weather faltered, and the storm ravaging the hollow broke. At once, the rain ceased and the black clouds parted. Above them, hanging in the night sky like a giant watching eye, the luminous moon was revealed.

Lord Walter approached his wretched sister, emboldened by the moonlight and by the demise of her possessed feline. 'Your demon is destroyed, and your familiar is dead. See sense and put an end to this madness!'

The Bloodstone

The glowing red orbs glided through the darkness. Snarls and guttural growls followed—and a stinking aroma akin to boiled cabbage and rotten meat.

'Raise swords!' Sir Vilfort cried, holding his own blade ready. Yet what were they defending themselves against? *I fear we will discover our fate all too soon.*

'How can we fight what we cannot see?' Sir Gilmore hissed through clenched teeth. The knight slashed his longsword into the blackness, frantically trying to deter whatever it was that came for them in the dark.

As the crimson orbs closed around them, shards of moonlight lanced into the mill through the broken shutters above. The light was weak but enough to discern the misshapen outlines of what assailed them. Bowlegged and long of limb, the things loomed from the shadows. Pig ugly and snarling with hatred, the sight of them was enough to make the knights wish the moonlight had not unveiled them at all. Brandishing axes, cudgels, and heavy curved butcher's blades designed for chopping meat and bone, the green-skins lurched from the gloom like formless wraiths, blurring in and out of existence as they passed through the shards of moonlight.

A dirty axe head buried itself into the centre of Sir Gilmore's shield. The shuddering thud sent a painful jolt through his body, numbing his arm. Grimacing, the knight lunged with his longsword, the blade sinking into soft green flesh. Howling in misery, the creature staggered away into the shadows, desperately trying to hold its writhing guts inside its bloated belly.

Sir Vilfort's blade sliced across a scrawny neck, splattering black blood over the lumber mill's timber walls. Then, blocking a rusty scimitar against his shield, he hacked a gangly arm from a green-skin's body, sending the warty appendage spiralling into the gloom.

Sir Richard grunted with discomfort. A powerful axe strike glanced from his shoulder guard spinning him sideways. Regaining his balance, the knight plunged with his longsword, skewering his ungodly perpetrator through the chest.

Sir Pottier swung at a pair of blood-red eyes. His blade sang through the darkness, slicing nothing except thin air. Then, from his blindside, a flash of movement. Immediately, he threw his shield up, but too late. A savage blow knocked him crashing to the ground. A deafening roaring filled his ears, and bitter blood spilt from his lips. Rolling onto his back, Sir Pottier spat a broken tooth through his helmet's now mangled faceguard.

Above him, the green-skin bent over his prone body with its cudgel poised. Bracing himself beneath his shield, Sir Pottier hoped to absorb the impact, but the cudgel failed to fall.

Banishing the shadows in its wake, a searing beam of light pulsed through the darkness condemning the fiend to oblivion and incinerating its sorry carcass into ash.

'Goblins,' Cassius hissed in disgust. 'I despise goblins!' With his energies rekindled by the luminous light of the moon, the angel once again gleamed white and gold, and as he strode forward to meet his foe, his sapphire eyes blazed with ice-cold malice.

'Filthy godforsaken wretches! They are the Devil's vermin! Slay them, Slay them all!' Consumed by battle lust—a questionable trait for an angelic legionary—the angel unleashed havoc upon the green-skin horde.

Possessed by rage, Cassius was unstoppable. His gleaming blade, reignited once more, was a swirling blur. He whirled and spun, a ballet of ruin, hewing green-skins into pieces as he clove a path deep into the mill.

The goblins were no match for an angel, especially not an angel bearing a psychotic grudge. They tried to flee. Some even made it past Cassius, but none escaped alive. If the shimmering sword failed to incinerate them, a bolt of angel light did the job.

Once the angel's brutal act of slaughter was over and the goblins' pleading screams had fallen silent, Cassius and the knights became aware of another presence within the lumber mill, a noise to lift their spirits and gladden their hearts.

Beneath a hatch in the floor, Darkham's children huddled together in the cold silent darkness of an underground cellar.

'Have no fear,' Cassius whispered softly. 'Nothing will harm you now. You are safe.'

Trembling, dirt-smeared faces stared from the pitch-black with haunted eyes. Warily at first and then with increasing desperation, the children climbed a rickety ladder into the arms of the waiting knights.

'Sir Pottier and Sir Richard, stay with the children,' Cassius instructed. Both knights had suffered injuries fighting the goblins, and although their wounds were not serious, the little ones required protection until it was safe to leave. 'It might be best if you keep your helmet on,' Cassius advised Sir Richard. 'The children have been through enough without having to look upon your face.'

Sir Richard nodded and knocked his faceguard into position. It was a fair statement. Although most of Darkham's younglings knew of his deformities, not all had seen his face for themselves and adding to their woes was a cruelness they could live without in the circumstances.

Cassius led Sir Vilfort and Sir Gilmore from the mill, their way lit by the angel's glowing aura. Outside, the storm had passed, and the moon shone above the hollow. It was a welcome sight for the knights, but the scene bathed within its pale light was not.

'What fresh evil is this?' Sir Vilfort despaired.

Slumped in the mud before the cottage, Lord Walter and his knights knelt at the witch's feet, seemingly enthralled by her power. A wavering otherworldly light drifted from their helpless bodies toward a strange red crystal atop Lady Margery's staff.

Overcome with rage, Sir Vilfort and Sir Gilmore began a haphazard charge across the slick terrain, determined to break the witch's spell and end her treacherous life once and for all with the cold steel of their longswords.

'Go no further,' Cassius warned. 'She will bewitch you with dark magic as she has done your comrades!'

Hell-bent on revenge, the two knights refused to listen, and as the angel had foreseen, Lady Margery's red magic pulsed to meet them, ensnaring them within its power just as it had done the others. Lord Walter and his men swayed back and forth, moaning in misery, their very essence draining to recharge Lady Margery's red crystal.

Cassius rolled his eyes. 'I have rid the world of a hell beast and a score of filth-ridden goblins, and now it seems I must slay a witch before my work is done,' he grumbled with contemptuous self-pity. *If I am not reassigned to a tropical paradise on completion of this assignment or, at the very least, the South of Frankia, I shall not be amused. Anywhere north of Paris would be an insult,* he decided with an affirmative nod. Gathering himself, he limped across the rainswept hollow, dreaming of feeling the hot sun on his back, the warm breeze on his face, and the soft touch of a scantily clad sand nymph on his lap. Yet first, the witch…

The answer to the angel's nagging riddle throbbed crimson at the end of the mad woman's stick. Here was the ancient evil at the heart of Greenwood, a thing of pure wickedness. *I had thought the red crystals all accounted for,* Cassius mused grimly. How the witch had acquired such a powerful artefact was puzzling.

Cassius moved quickly. He knew a bloodstone of the size the witch possessed could leech the life force from Lord Walter and his knights in mere moments. 'The witch is playing with fire,' the angel grunted. *And everyone knows what happens if you play with fire. You get burnt to a crisp.* It was time to dispense God's justice and unleash the cleansing flames of Heaven upon her. *In other words, the heathen hag is going to roast.*

Cassius drank moonlight like an elixir, absorbing the energy through his skin until he felt its magnificence surging inside his veins. Bursting with new power, he discharged a crackling torrent of angel light, the white-hot energy lancing through the dank hollow, lighting the night sky with its brilliance.

Lady Margery swung to face the blast of holy light, releasing her hold over the men of Darkham in doing so. Like a writhing crimson fog, the life force that lay thick and heavy about the cottage began returning to its hosts, seeping back into the knights' bodies and restoring their withering souls.

Calling upon the bloodstone's dark powers, the witch retaliated. Red light met white between the lumber mill and the cottage, and as the opposing columns of energy collided, they exploded in an eruption of swirling colours and roaring flame.

The force of the witch's magic rocked Cassius onto his heels, pushing him back through the mud. Yet, with the moon shining brightly above, he drew upon its power, channelling more and more energy through his outstretched hands. Now it was the witch's turn to be forced onto the defensive. The howling stream of crimson flame spewing from Lady Margery's staff began receding across the hollow, retreating against the brilliance of the angel's might.

The witch was close to breaking; Cassius could feel her hellfire faltering. *Just a little longer.* Suddenly, intense pain exploded through his body, a jolting blow causing the angel to arch his back and scream to the heavens in agony. Uncontrolled, the angel light streaking from his hands swept into the night sky, slashing the cottage in two before blinking out altogether. The witch's hellfire continued unopposed, blazing past the stricken angel by a hair's breadth to set the lumber mill alight.

Only a weapon fortified by dark magic or devilry or one that has been forged in Heaven or Hell is capable of inflicting injury upon the Almighty's immortal legionaries. Yet, the black-bladed dagger protruding from the angel's side was such a device. The goblin yanked the weapon free and, grinning with relish, rammed the cursed blade home again. Cassius screamed anew, falling into the mire upon his knees.

Lady Margery's face beamed, her black soul swelling with joy. 'Oh, what a wonderful creature you are,' she called, praising her green-skinned ally's excellent work. Summoning the elements once more, the witch manipulated the winds, driving thick impenetrable clouds to conceal the moon and darken the sky. 'I forbid you access to the light, angel.'

Grasping Cassius from behind, the filthy goblin held the tainted blade firmly inside the angel's body, buried deep between his ribs. Agonising pain throbbed mercilessly from the wound. Cassius felt the weapon pulsing with unholy power, corrupting his flesh, seeping into his veins. The proximity of the reeking green-skin was fuel enough to ignite the angel's rage, but his poisoned muscles refused to obey. Try as he might, he failed to muster the strength to strike the goblin down and dislodge the dagger. *I shall fade and die if the cursed blade is not soon removed.*

A second jet of red light hurtled toward him, and in that awful moment, Cassius realised he was defenceless. In all honesty, he was more than a little irked to be meeting his end in this way. *Defeated at the hands of an amateur witch in a sodden English wood.* 'As God wills it,' he muttered wryly. This was not how Cassius envisaged his death. Forever had he pictured himself happy and fat, having spent a comfortable retirement bathed in Heaven's light, drifting contentedly into blessed oblivion whilst serenaded by a bevy of naked lady angels—that or going down in a blaze of glory fighting against the Devil and all the hosts of Hell… whilst, of course, attempting to rescue a bevy of naked lady angels. *Anything but this,* he moaned dismally.

Nonetheless, when the red light struck, Cassius quickly realised that for now—in the absence of burning flame and smouldering flesh—his end had not come but was merely delayed. The dark magic pulsing from the witch's staff was, in actuality, the same spell she had cast upon Lord Walter and his knights. Cassius concluded rather forlornly that his situation had not improved despite this fortuitous development. *I have swapped instant incineration for a slow, torturous death by leeching.* And worse than that, by stealing the angel's life force Lady Margery's power would increase tenfold.

The crimson energy surged around him, cocooning him within an unbreakable sphere of evil. 'If it rains, it pours,' the angel mumbled miserably. Indeed, no sooner had Cassius uttered the phrase did the clouds above the hollow begin emptying themselves again and with no less enthusiasm than before.

Abruptly, Cassius lurched forward. The witch's red light dragged him toward her, hauling him through the mud and filth on his knees. Lady Margery felt the angel's life force flooding into the bloodstone. She cared not that the lumber mill was ablaze nor that her precious captives were fleeing into the safety of the winter wood. She only cared for the intoxicating torrent of pure energy pouring into her crystal-tipped staff. She sensed its magnificence as it flowed through her, an endless river of power. *Now I can summon not one but a hundred demons!* First, she would overthrow King Edward, and once England had fallen, she would claim Europe, and the entire world would follow!

Agony contorted Lady Margery's features. Horrified, she stared down to see cold steel sticking from her belly, put there by none other than Lord Walter, her beloved brother. Realisation drained the life from her twisted features, and within her broken body, her darkened soul writhed in turmoil. The witch's dreams were shattered, and she was going to Hell.

'Goodbye, Sister,' Lord Walter whispered, pushing his blade deeper inside her body.

Screaming one last time, Lady Margery sagged into her brother's arms, a final embrace before darkness claimed her.

Epilogue

The following day, with sunlight at their backs and good cheer in their hearts, Lord Walter and his knights led the children of Darkham home. Father Gilda proclaimed it a day of miracles, a Christmas never to be forgotten.

'But, Lord, where is the crusader?' Where is Sir Cassius?' Mary Windle had asked, holding her children close.

Lord Walter shook his head. 'I know not,' he said. 'There was no sign of him once the witch was slain.' For a moment, his face lightened. 'I think his work was done, and he returned whence he came. Alas, he departed without telling his story. I would have believed every word.'

Meanwhile, in the shade of Greenwood…

Laid low by his wound, Cassius hunched in the saddle. 'Horse, my friend,' he muttered feebly, patting the animal's flank with affection, 'take me into the light.'

Whickering softly, the steed dutifully carried his injured passenger from the dark embrace of the trees and into the wonderous glare of the rising sun.

Later at the hollow…

Like a rabid hound with the scent of blood in its nostrils, the goblin dug feverishly in the mud. He knew it was here somewhere. He had seen it fall from the witch's grasp, and now it called to him from beneath the sludge.

At last, the green-skin's wart-ridden fingers felt something buried deep within the filth, something hard. Frantically, the creature pulled it free. A blood-red crystal. Hugging the precious treasure against its black heart, the goblin hurried into the dark woods to find its master.

~ The End ~

Demon Hunters

The Chronicles of Cassius

~ Titan Fall ~

The North Atlantic Ocean, 1912

The world's grandest passenger liner, RMS Titanic, steams toward New York.

Winslow and Grace are to be married on their return to England, but they must first survive history's most infamous maritime disaster.

Cassius is torn between doing his duty, settling an old score, and saving lives.

Demon Hunters

Heroic Fantasy through the Ages

Last of the Kraken

Deep beneath the surface of the Atlantic Ocean, five glowing lights illuminated the dark, fathomless depths. Homing in on their unholy prey, the angels sped through the ice-cold waters like gleaming torpedoes.

Lurching into the gloom, the demon fled, its vast bulk a sprawling shadow, an immense storm front rolling silently into the murky distance.

Manakel, Angel of the Seven Seas, led the underwater charge and swiftly did he and his brethren gain on their monstrous foe. Gleaming like stars, the angels summoned their divine power, ready to strike. But then, the sea creature was gone.

No, not gone, merely hidden from view, Cassius mused.

Suddenly, darkness surged at them, a tumultuous underwater thundercloud threatening to consume everything in its path.

Oh, wonderous. Nothing strips flesh from bone faster than kraken ink.

The angels split apart, sweeping around the churning swell of toxic discharge that seethed menacingly in the pitch-black depths.

Cassius wasn't sure if the kraken's rear looked any prettier than its front, and if not for the creature's two huge crimson eyes that glowed in the dark like blazing rings of fire, he would have struggled to tell face from arse altogether.

Karnakoor, the last of Leviathan's children. Such a handsome devil. In truth, the sea titans had seldom looked anything but grotesque. *Yet Karnakoor appears impressively hideous, and I can see he has grown fat with age.*

Earth's oceans are deep and vast, and there are places below the waves untouched by light—immense bottomless sea trenches as black as death where no human or angel dare go.

The perfect hideout for villainous squid.

Three days ago, while navigating the North Atlantic ice flow, a herd of humpbacked whales were savagely attacked. Investigating their decimated remains, Manakel's suspicions were confirmed: the last of the kraken had re-emerged.

Fifty years without a meal makes Karnakoor a hungry boy, Cassius mused wryly. Gathering his energies, the angel shone with power. *Speaking of food, how I adore fried calamari!*

Angel light flashed from his hands into the darkness, a crackling column of jolting energy. Cassius watched other blasts of light join his own, streaking through the water.

The holy missiles struck the monster's glistening green hide, flaring bright one after the other. Consumed by terrible rage, the beast twisted its enormous, bloated frame to face its tormentors. Giant snaking tentacles uncoiled with venomous speed, each a flailing club adorned with poisonous suckers and barbs.

Zadkiel was lashed deep down amidst the ocean's gloomy depths, and Neos smashed into the distant murk. Ducking and diving, Manakel and Sachael eluded the tentacles, but as Cassius closed ranks with his angel brethren, the demon's gaping maw opened. A booming roar spewed from within its vile innards, striking the angels like an invisible tsunami.

Cassius felt himself spiralling through the water at great speed. His ears screamed, his head pounded, and every inch of his body groaned. It was as if he'd been bludgeoned by an enormous cannonball.

Eventually, Cassius slowed, and his senses returned. *That was something of a schoolboy error. Next time, it would be wise to avoid the demon's charms. Manakel ought to have remembered the titan's many forms of defence, not least its sonic pulse. How long has the pompous fool hunted the damnable fish?* Manakel pulled rank here only because he was the so-called *Angel of the Seven Seas.* Well, he could keep his aquatic friends. The sooner they fried Karnakoor, the sooner Cassius could return to dry land. *The smell of kipper will doubtlessly linger for weeks*, he moaned. *God, I hate the ocean, and I hate Manakel more.*

Cassius darted through the sea, his angel wings propelling him onwards like supersonic underwater oars. Ahead, the glow of his brethren called him. Nursing their bruised egos and bodies, the angels gathered themselves, regrouping before continuing the monster hunt.

'The beast craves sustenance,' Manakel explained. 'To fill his belly, he is drawn to the shipping lanes. If Karnakoor reaches those ships, I do not need to tell you what will happen.'

An all-you-can-eat buffet, Cassius thought grimly.

The other angels bowed their heads in sombre reflection.

'Well, then, what are we waiting for?' Cassius said, stirring his brethren into action. 'If we are to prevent a tragedy, we don't have a moment to lose.'

A Sky Full of Stars

'Some of the chaps are arranging a game of cricket up on deck in the morning,' Winslow Selsby said, slurping tea from a Royal Crown Derby cup and saucer. 'Although I'm not entirely sure I'll be in any sort of state to participate.' Concentrating intently, he successfully returned the bone China cup and saucer to the table without spilling a drop of the contents. He grinned inanely at his achievement.

'Well, you only have yourself to blame, Winnie,' Grace replied. 'Rum versus your liver invariably ends in tears. You know full well that your constitution is less manly than it ought to be.'

Raising an eyebrow, Winslow stared at his fiancée in mock horror. 'My darling, your words are a dagger through my heart!' Much to his betrothed's embarrassment, Winslow clutched his chest and feigned a dramatic death sequence, complete with screams and gurgles.

Grace glanced furtively at the other guests taking their post-dinner rest in the ship's first-class reception room. 'Stop it, you fool!' she pleaded, desperately trying to suppress a fit of giggles from squirming out of her mouth. Winslow was such an idiot. And he certainly didn't act anything like he should. His father was a lord, a man of wealth and standing. Winnie was in line to inherit enough cash to buy anything he wanted: a London retreat, a French vineyard, a West Indian island, an Aboriginal tribe… Nothing would ever be too much again.

'My apologies,' Winslow said, fiddling with his dickie-bow as if he expected a jet of water to squirt his fiancée in the face. 'The ruddy thing isn't working,' he mumbled before sniggering drunkenly. 'It seems I'm too foolish by half, my dear. At least I am for this assemblage of crashing bores and spoilsports.'

The other guests glared at him with hunched brows and disapproving stares. Even the resident pianist had interrupted his sombre key tinkering to add a disgruntled scowl.

Grace was mortified. 'Sssshhh! I beg you, Winnie!' She didn't dare raise her gaze any higher than the teacups on the table for fear of catching a fellow passenger's eye. *What must they be thinking?* 'Come,' she said to Winslow. 'Fresh air is your only cure. And if that fails, well, there is always the Atlantic Ocean. A well-timed push will put an end to your foolishness.'

'You wouldn't dare!'

The pair pushed back their chairs and stood. 'I would, and you know it,' Grace said, winking mischievously.

Winslow narrowed his eyes. 'I believe you would.' Grinning proudly, his gaze sunk to Grace's belly. She wore a full-length chiffon gown of citron ornamented with beads and lace and complemented with a long mink scarf strategically positioned to hide her condition. 'Please forgive my overindulgence, my dear, but soon I fear the patter of tiny feet will put an end to my frivolities once and for all.'

Grace sniggered. 'I'll hold you to that, darling. However, if your friends are an example—Bertie, Titch… and who's that other? The one with the gammy leg? Fudger! That's him—I expect your *frivolities* to increase, not decline.'

Straightening his dickie and correcting his posture, which was listing precariously to starboard, Winslow composed himself as well as could be managed. 'I am not like my friends,' he declared staunchly. However, the sincerity of the moment was compromised by an involuntary and violent bout of hiccups.

Shaking her head, Grace grabbed her fiancé's hand. 'Come on, away with you. We have disturbed these good people for long enough. A lungful of icy air and then to bed.'

Leading Winslow between the sour-faced guests who slouched post supper like bloated hogs wedged into their seats at their tables, Grace ushered him onto the stairs, heading to the upper decks.

The Grand Staircase aboard RMS Titanic would not have been out of place in a stately home or royal palace. Crafted from the finest English oak, the lavish construction spanned six decks and was a marvel to behold.

Ascending arm in arm with her betrothed, Grace couldn't help peering upwards as she'd done countless times since leaving port at Southampton. Above, crowning the beautiful staircases' sweeping curves, was a magnificent glass dome. A sparkling chandelier hung at its centre like a shining star in the heavens. 'This ship is really something,' she whispered, passing beneath.

Titanic was like a floating hotel, like the Ritz out at sea. At least, it was for the wealthy. Sometimes it was easy to forget that the gigantic vessel was a ship at all. Grace counted herself incredibly blessed to be part of Titanic's maiden voyage. Being engaged to Winslow Selsby had significantly improved her fortunes. And even though she found the upper classes a very peculiar breed indeed, coexisting amidst such finery and amongst such important, well-educated people was like living in a wondrous dream. Her only concern was waking to discover none of it was real.

Naturally, Winnie's father, Lord Selsby, hadn't endorsed the match. He would have preferred his only son to have chosen a partner better suited to his station. The Earl of Wimbourne's daughter, Lady Felicity Bracegirdle or Lord Hussie's niece, Lady Penelope Parpington. Either would have sufficed, honourable, decent folk who owned half of England between them.

Grace smiled. Lord Selsby hadn't approved, but Winnie's mother, Lady Anne Selsby, certainly had. From the first moment they met, she and Grace got on like a house on fire. And as most men are governed by their good ladies, at least in matters of the heart, her decision was final. This once-in-a-lifetime ocean voyage was an engagement gift from Winnie's parents. First-class cabins and every luxury included.

Little do they know of the surprise I carry inside me, Grace mused slyly. In the circumstances, her betrothed had hastily arranged the wedding for their return from New York. *I cannot wait to see Lord Selsby's face once he realises his grandchild has come too early.*

'Goodness gracious me,' Winslow blurted, stumbling to a stop halfway up the staircase. A beautifully carved panel faced him and at its wooden heart was an ornate clock face. 'Half-past eleven! Whatever has happened to the evening, my dear?'

Grace rolled her eyes. 'It has vanished, Winnie, along with the contents of a bottle of rum at supper,' she replied, dragging her fiancé upwards.

Once outside, Grace helped Winslow onto the promenade and then across to the starboard handrail. 'Here we are,' she announced. 'The night is fresh enough to clear the most pickled of heads.'

Gripping the cold iron bar, Winslow peered over the edge. The water rushing beneath him made his head spin. He gulped down great mouthfuls of air as if his life depended on the volume of oxygen inhaled. 'In truth, my darling, now that I am out here, I feel decidedly worse.'

Grace snorted. 'You'll get no sympathy from me,' she said, staring into the night. The view was like nothing she had seen before. 'What an enchanting spectacle.' The water appeared like an endless sheet of black glass, so smooth and still that the numberless stars in the sky reflected perfectly upon its surface. 'Look, Winnie, we float amongst the heavens.'

Stationed within the vessel's crow's nest high above the couple—the best position to spot pretty passengers, aquatic acrobats, sensational sunsets, and suspicious lumps of ice—a lookout noticed a perplexing haze on the horizon. 'What do you make of that, Stan?' Frank asked his colleague, straining his eyes to see into the darkness.

The temperature had plummeted since nightfall. The cold was bitter a hundred feet above deck. Stan rubbed at his hands, frantically trying to warm them. 'Probably nowt.' To be honest, Stan had absolutely no idea what he was supposed to be looking at. He couldn't see anything except millions of bleeding stars.

'We're entering Iceberg Alley,' Frank said. 'Keep your eyes peeled.'

Captain Smith had warned his lookouts to remain vigilant throughout the night. Striking an iceberg was far from ideal, but seldom did a vessel end up on the bottom of the seabed as a result. Modern ocean liners were designed to survive impacts, and no ship was designed more meticulously than Titanic. Nonetheless, Frank and Stan were taking no chances. The men searched the starlit waters ceaselessly, watching the shadowed horizon that blurred and shimmered before them.

Winslow and Grace found themselves alone. The other guests had gone to their beds, and now the couple had the promenade to themselves. Any thoughts of retiring for the evening were forgotten. At least they were for Grace.

'Are you feeling any better, darling?' she inquired, studying her betrothed thoughtfully. After a moment, Grace nodded with approval. His eyes were clearer, the swaying had ceased, and his desire to eject the contents of his stomach overboard had seemingly receded. 'I rather fancy a stroll along the promenade. The sky is delightful this evening, don't you think?

And the sea is so serene. Please, Winnie, indulge me. If only for a few minutes.'

Winslow executed an elaborate bow. 'As you command, my Lady,' he said, linking arms with Grace once more.

The couple set off, admiring a sky full of stars as they walked. They passed Café Parisian, where rows of deckchairs were lined up outside, ready for the morning sun. The venue was ever a popular destination during the day. *If Winnie is feeling up to it, perhaps we shall come for breakfast before he plays cricket with the chaps.* Grace smiled. She couldn't remember feeling so content. *A perfect evening,* she thought happily.

Somewhere a bell rang. Not once, but three times. Then, quite suddenly, the ship lurched violently to port.

Stumbling across the width of the walkway, Grace and Winslow quickly found themselves pressed against the iron railings. The pair held on for dear life while Titanic's abrupt change in direction persisted.

'What's happening, Winnie?' Grace demanded breathlessly.

'I really don't know,' Winslow confessed, ensuring he had a firm grip of Grace.

In answer, a voice somewhere above them yelled into the night. 'Iceberg! Dead ahead!'

The chill air caught in Grace's throat, and a rush of fear surged through her veins.

'Don't worry, I'm sure we'll miss the brute,' Winslow said reassuringly, squeezing Grace's hands.

Seconds later, the ship rocked again, and for a few moments after, there came a juddering moan from starboard, a grating sensation that felt as if they were rolling over a giant cattle grid.

Immediately afterwards, Titanic righted herself, and all seemed well.

Grace and Winslow stared into one another's wide, frightened eyes.

'Why have the engines stopped?' Winslow whispered.

Beneath the Waves

Beneath the shimmering waterline, angel light blasted Karnakoor's tentacles from Titanic's hull. The demon's wicked barbed hooks had torn open the ship, and now tons of seawater gushed inside. The monster unleashed its sonic roar against its enemies, but this time Manakel and his brethren were long gone before the deafening pulse could strike them.

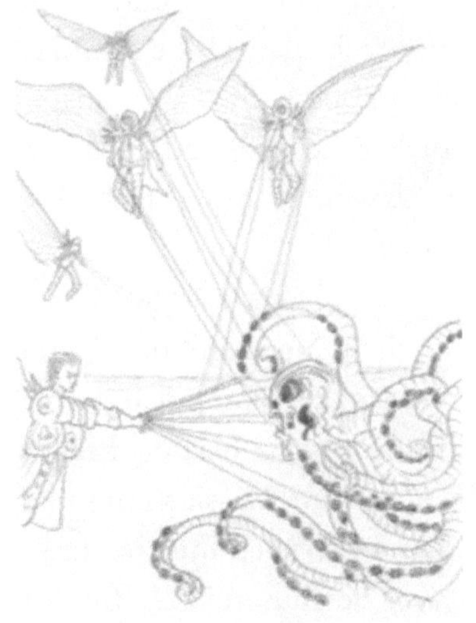

The angels pummelled the beast with blast after blast of sizzling energy. Then, when the titan's attention was drawn, they darted out of harm's way. Repeating the tactic, they lured the monster from the wounded vessel. But Karnakoor learned fast. Zadkiel found himself ensnared by a waiting tentacle. The appendage reeled him toward a cavernous mouth, where a multitude of leech-like tendrils writhed with eagerness for the taste of angel flesh.

'Zadkiel is captured. The kraken anticipates our plans!' Manakel called to his angels.

Zadkiel was helpless, he pulsed with holy light, blistering the monster's green hide, but it wasn't enough. His limbs were immobilised. Oozing toxic slime burned his skin. Zadkiel was carried closer to the beast's dreadful glowing red eyes and the wide-open abyss waiting for him.

Suddenly, a gleaming white light shone through the water, striking the creature's misshapen bulk. Surging through the murky depths, Zadkiel's brethren had come to his aid. Cassius and Neos bombarded the titan with pulsing spheres of light that crackled and hissed as they zipped through the deep. Manakel and Sachael tackled the monstrous limb holding their brother within its coiled grasp. The angels blasted the arm-like stem until it writhed. Manakel grabbed the appendage, wrestling its vice-like grip apart. Stuck as he was, Zadkiel could offer no assistance. The demon unwound more tentacles, launching them like freakish harpoons.

'Incoming!' Manakel warned.

Sachael was captured first, and then Neos. Manakel and Cassius defied the demon's efforts. Manakel manipulated holy light, sculpting the power into the form of a blazing trident which he thrust at the tentacle assailing him. Cassius conjured a shield, using the shining golden barrier to keep the creature's limbs at bay. *A persistent squid indeed*, he mused. Yet, five of Karnakoor's eight terrible appendages remained free to do the demon's bidding, and five against two were unfavourable odds.

Manakel lunged, spearing his trident deep into the flesh of a tentacle. 'Feel my wrath, devil-spawn!' The thing jerked away from the blow. The angel pursued the stricken limb, keen to press home his advantage. He surged to intercept but was struck from behind. A second tentacle coiled around the angel's torso, wrapping itself tighter and tighter. 'Alas, the foul thing has me!'

Cassius alone endured, but now three of the demon's flailing arms crashed against his defences, a relentless pounding threatening to shatter the angel's holy shield into a million shards of light. *Why is it always me who must save the day? And never am I thanked for my efforts.*

Karnakoor hauled its prisoners toward its gruesome mouth. Pinned by suckers and barbs, they could do nothing to escape their dreadful fate. Yet Manakel was the Angel of the Seven Seas, and now he called upon the many creatures of the ocean, summoning them to his side.

'Fear not, my brethren,' Manakel's voice boomed through the water. 'My friends are here to aid us in our time of need!'

Legions of great white sharks emerged into the light radiating from the glowing angels. From every direction, the cold-blooded killers launched themselves in a frenzied assault. Hundreds of razor-sharp teeth began tearing chunks of green flesh from the beast's vast torso.

Frantically redeploying its tentacles, the kraken sought to rip the sharks from its body. Free from Karnakoor's attentions, Cassius propelled himself toward the demon's monstrous face. *Ah, ha! Cassius to the rescue once again!*

Manakel and his brethren were moments from being deposited into the immense black vacuum that loomed ahead. Spewing from deep within Karnakoor's innards, the repugnant scent of death greeted their arrival. 'Prepare yourselves for oblivion!' Manakel cried.

Cassius directed a streaking bolt of angel light straight into the beast's gaping maw, but the attack did little to deter the beast.

'Give me your power!' Cassius called to his brethren, hurling everything he had at the titan. Crackling energy shot like laser beams from his hands.

Manakel pulsed with power, and so did Zadkiel, Neos, and Sachael. Wavering lines of gleaming light seeped from their bodies, drifting through the ocean currents to merge with Cassius.

'Now!' Manakel cried. 'Use our strength before we are cast into Hell!'

For a split second, Cassius hesitated. He pictured Manakel's broken body disappearing inside the kraken. *Tempting, but I would never forgive myself.* Actually, he probably would, but the powers that be certainly wouldn't. *Why must I suffer fools gladly*, he moaned.

In a tidal wave of shimmering energy, Cassius unleashed the unified power of five angels. An immense singular column of burning white-hot angel light detonated inside Karnakoor.

The colossal beast wailed in despair. Releasing its prey, its squirming tentacles retracted, coiling protectively around its great bulk. Slowly, the red-eyed monstrosity sank into the Atlantic's fathomless depths. The angels watched as the creature disappeared deep into the gloom.

'Cassius, the humans' sea vessel is damaged, do what you can to help,' Manakel instructed. 'The rest of us will finish this.'

Manakel, the Angel of the Seven Seas, led Zadkiel, Neos, Sachael, and a mighty armada of great white sharks after the titan.

'Sea vessel? Who says *sea vessel* these days? And not once did the ungrateful swine thank me,' Cassius muttered to himself as he sped toward Titanic.

At the bottom of the deep blue sea, where the dark is king and the cold is queen, the giant kraken stirred. Slumped forlornly upon the seabed, he waited, and through the smallest of cracks between the tentacles wrapped tightly around his bulbous head, he watched. Unbeknown to Manakel and his angels, Karnakoor was far from beaten.

Intent on his destruction, the angels and their allies came for him. Yet lured so easily to the bottom of the ocean, it was they who would be destroyed.

All at once, the titan's dormant limbs burst apart and from its yawning maw exploded a booming wave of sonic energy to blast the sea monster's enemies far and wide.

Captain Cassius

Grace and Winslow sped along the promenade, climbed up and over the Boat Deck and headed to the ship's prow.

'If we struck an iceberg, then where is it?' Grace said. The couple hauled themselves onto the railings and peered overboard. 'There's nothing out there.'

Out of nowhere, a man appeared beside the couple. 'What do you see?'

The fellow was dressed in uniform: black and white cap, navy-blue double-breasted jacket, crisp white shirt, narrow black necktie, pressed navy-blue trousers, and well-polished black leather shoes. He was a crewman and, by the look of him, an officer.

'Nothing,' Winslow answered, trying his utmost not to appear as tipsy or queasy as he felt—nor as foolish as his dearest Grace expected. 'What has happened, my good man?'

Ignoring Winslow's question, the officer mounted the railings to see for himself. 'There's no sign of an iceberg,' he muttered, more for his own benefit than Grace or Winslow's. 'Perhaps there's an ice shelf beneath the surface. Either way, we hit something, and now our hull is compromised.'

'Compromised?' Grace questioned with a troubled frown. 'What do you mean, *compromised?*' It was a word that filled her with dread, and even as she uttered it, the ship began listing to starboard.

The officer stepped down from the railings. 'Take my advice, madame,' he said gravely. 'Say a prayer and be ready by the lifeboats.'

Winslow had never sobered up so fast. 'She's sinking? You can't be serious, man? The greatest ocean liner of her age doomed by invisible ice. I won't believe it, sir, not for a second!'

The officer didn't reply, nor did he need to; the expression on his face was answer enough. 'I must return to the bridge.'

A blur of movement caused them to cradle their heads and drop to the deck. Grace caught sight of a huge shadow whooshing over their heads. A loud squelching thump was preceded by a shower of seawater that soaked them like a mini monsoon. Dripping wet, Grace, Winslow, and the officer swivelled their heads to stare.

An enormous and very much dead great white shark lay upon the deck. Lost for words and drawn by a terrible curiosity, the three crept nearer. A horrific wound raked the shark's flank. But how—even without accounting for its awful injury or the fact that it was unquestionably deceased—had the sea creature ended up aboard Titanic?

'There are sixty feet between us and the water,' the officer said, shaking his head. 'Never in all my years at sea have I witnessed such a thing.'

Beneath them, another boom rocked the ship. Not a jarring noise like before, but a sudden bang, like a depth charge exploding a hundred fathoms under the sea. Then, just for an instant, the night sky was lit with such fierceness it stung their eyes.

'By all things holy, what the hell is going on?' Winslow Selsby exclaimed.

As darkness descended once more, a second officer materialised seemingly from thin air. He began observing the peculiar addition to the ship's passenger list, or so it seemed to those already pondering the bizarre interloper.

The man's uniform matched the officer's. However, instead of two golden stripes upon his jacket sleeves, four wrapped the cuff, and the last was looped just as it was on Captain Smith's uniform.

'She's a big girl,' the captain stated.

At first, Grace wondered if the man was referring to her, but of course, he meant the shark. 'Yes,' she said. 'For the life of me, I never thought to see a great white and certainly not in such proximity.' Any closer, and she risked swooning.

'Indeed,' the captain said, and then he did something strange. He bent down at the shark's side and laid a hand gently on the creature's fin. He mumbled words that Grace couldn't make out, but she definitely heard something about a 'brave Sacrifice'. *Why would he say that?*

Stepping from the shark's hulking corpse, the captain went briskly about his business. 'What's the situation?' he asked the officer.

'We've hit something. In all probability, an ice shelf beneath the surface. The ship is taking on water at a frightful rate. Several compartments are in the process of flooding.'

'Show me,' said the captain.

The officer hesitated. 'Forgive me for saying so, sir, but I cannot recall your name? In all honesty, I cannot recall having seen you at all before tonight.'

The man smiled and offered his hand for shaking. 'No, we haven't met. My name is Captain Cassius, and you are Jamie Monroe, if I'm not mistaken?'

Monroe nodded, accepting the captain's hand.

'The Navy and I have parted company,' Cassius explained. 'We are sick of the sight of one another,' he added in the way of an explanation, all be it a rather vague one. 'Instead, I have kindly been offered a captaincy aboard a White Star Line vessel. This voyage was intended to aid my transition from the Navy. In preparation for my command, I was to observe Captain Smith's methods, but now it seems he needs my help. So my good fellow, let me help. Show me the flooded compartments.'

'Of course, sir.'

Cassius shifted his attention to Grace and Winslow. 'You two, make yourselves useful,' he said. 'Aid Captain Smith and his crew. Rouse the passengers. Bring them up on deck. In the meantime, I'll see what can be done below.'

Leaving the mauled shark behind them, they hastened along the length of Titanic's superstructure passing beneath the first of the vessel's four giant black-topped funnels, three of which belched steam into the night sky. Reaching midships, where the raised roof of the first-class lounge protruded skyward before them, they ducked through a sliding door leading to the Grand

Staircase. Arriving on B-Deck's landing, the group parted ways. Compelled to help the captain, Grace and Winslow were determined to rouse Titanic's passengers from their cabins.

Meanwhile, Monroe led Cassius ever deeper into the vessel's lower levels. The staircase terminated on F-Deck but darting along a corridor and then down another flight of stairs, they were soon within Titanic's bowels. They hurried past the boiler rooms until they reached the furthest forward. Before pulling open the watertight door, Cassius paused. 'How many flooded compartments can the ship endure?'

'Five, sir,' Monroe replied.

'And are all the compartments compromised beyond this point?'

Monroe nodded grimly. 'Yes, the squash court and cargo holds one, two, and three.'

Cassius wrenched open the door and leapt through. 'Then the fifth compartment must be saved.'

Mayhem greeted them. From deep below rose the sounds of roaring furnaces, the whistling squeal of vented steam, and the cries of desperate engineers.

'Quickly, while we still have time,' Cassius said. Like a snakes and ladders board, a network of iron-wrought ladders and twisting pipes disappeared into the depths. Ignoring the conventional way down, Cassius launched himself from the upper platform. Preserving his identity was no longer a priority, not when so many souls were in danger.

'What on earth are you doing, man?' Monroe cried, horrified. But the captain was already gone. Rushing across the platform, the officer peered over the edge. He couldn't see anything through the steam and smoke billowing below him. 'Good

God. Why would he do such a thing?' With his heart pounding, he swung himself onto the ladder and began clambering down.

Below, Cassius splashed into water. It was knee-high and rising fast, but it wasn't too late. *I'll put this right in a jiffy*. All that was required was a little patience and some expert welding.

The boiler room was chaos. As the Atlantic Ocean poured through a ragged scar torn into the ship's mighty hull, firemen and stokers worked feverishly to stem the rising tide and suppress the furnaces. Ice-cold seawater meeting red-hot coal is an ill-advised union, usually resulting in things exploding rather violently.

'We douse the fires and vent the boilers as fast as can be managed. If the water gets too high and the furnaces are flooded, we'll have a bigger hole to worry about than that little scrape along the keel,' Mr Barrett, the lead stoker, declared.

'Valiant work, my friend,' Cassius replied. 'I'll not keep you from your task.'

The stoker, soaked to the bone and smeared head to toe in soot and grime, eyed the captain grimly. 'The water rushes aboard faster than we can pump.' He shook his head sadly. 'We can't save her, can we, sir?'

Cassius watched the steam and smoke as it coiled upwards. 'The chamber is high,' he said. 'We have time.'

'Begging my pardon, sir, but the hull will need repairing if the water is to be stopped.'

Cassius smiled. 'Precisely, Mr Barrett, and that is what shall be done.'

Barrett snorted with derision. 'No offence, Captain, but you're mad if you believe the ship can be patched up.' Having heard enough, the lead stoker waded through the ever-rising seawater to rejoin his men dousing the fires.

By the time Monroe descended the many ladders to reach the bottom, the water swelled ominously about the captain's waistline. 'How did you leap from so high and live? Do you have the wings of a bird, sir?'

Cassius chuckled. 'No, not a bird, Mr Monroe.'

Monroe frowned. Something wasn't right. In the circumstances, he decided against debating the peculiar episode further. It was entirely plausible, pushed to the limits as he was, that his mind was playing tricks on him. 'What do you hope to achieve down here, sir?'

'Titanic's salvation,' Cassius replied. 'Aid the firemen and stokers, and when their jobs are done, retreat from the chamber, securing the door behind you.'

'What about you, Captain?'

'I will remain until my task is complete.'

Monroe nodded. In truth, he was far from sure what Captain Cassius planned or hoped to gain by staying behind, and he half suspected the man had lost his mind. After all, once the door was secured, there would be no escape.

The gash in Titanic's side extended along a three-hundred-foot stretch. It wasn't one continuous rip but a succession of smaller openings, and here in boiler room six, those openings were now below the waterline.

Plunging into the cold murk, Cassius surveyed the damage. *The fat kraken's hooks have ripped the ship open like a can of sardines. It was fortunate he wasn't given a chance to reach within and pluck out the tasty morsels hiding inside.*

The onrushing ocean was a force to be reckoned with, a relentless surging power Cassius could barely stand against. Yet stand he did. What's more, illuminating the gloom with angel light, he began super-heating the buckled section of hull where the damaged metal was bent inwards by the kraken's hooks. Piece by piece, the angel manipulated the twisted lumps of iron back into position. The task was slow and laborious, and Cassius was painfully aware of the time he was taking. It was a remedial chore for an angel blessed with Cassius's skill set. Once again, he was proving his undoubted devotion to humanity… and his desire for redemption and a lovely retirement bathed in Heaven's everlasting light. *Have I not done enough to earn my place? Surely I have atoned for my mistakes?*

The seawater bubbled and hissed as angel light sealed the breach. Having repaired the first opening, Cassius pushed himself from the hull and surged upwards through the churning seawater. With three holes remaining, he needed to ensure sufficient time to complete the job before the water reached the boiler room's open bulkhead and began flooding the next compartment. Bobbing to the surface, the angel's suspicions were confirmed. The water had all but reached the door.

Monroe and Barrett stood atop the uppermost platform, urging the last of the crew to safety. Monroe pointed into the turbulent waters below. 'Look, it's the captain!'

Barrett couldn't believe his eyes. 'God's teeth, you're right. Quickly, sir, before it's too late!'

'Seal the door, gentlemen,' Cassius replied. 'My task is not yet done.'

Both Monroe and Barrett stared at the captain in disbelief.

'Don't be a fool,' Barrett argued.

'If we seal the door, you'll be trapped inside, sir,' Monroe explained, dismayed by the captain's ridiculous refusal to abandon a lost cause. But even before the officer's warning was spoken, Cassius had vanished beneath the frothing surface. 'What's he doing?'

Barrett shoved Monroe through the door. 'Leave him,' Barrett said. 'He's a dead man.'

Abandon Ship!

'Are you drunk?' Lady Farthingdale demanded, scrunching up her age-wrinkled features with indignation. 'The unsinkable ship sinking. Absolute claptrap.'

Grace opened her mouth to protest, but the old woman was having none of it.

'If waking us at this ungodly hour isn't bad enough,' the old woman nagged, wagging an accusing digit in a very intimidating fashion, 'you then have the gall to scare us both half to death with stories of doom and gloom.' Lady Farthingdale flung a robbed arm in the general direction of her husband, Lord Farthingdale. By the expression on his withered prune-like face, he was finding the incident highly entertaining. 'Why, only this evening, Mr Andrews, the ship's grand architect, who I might add is a dear friend, was informing Lord Farthingdale of Titanic's many virtues, foremost of which is her robust construction. So you see, knowing what I know makes you liars… or drunks!' Then she thought for a moment. 'Or drunk liars!'

Employing a surprisingly stiff index finger, she began poking and prodding the intruders backwards toward the door. 'Now get out of my cabin before I have the staff throw you overboard like a pair of stowaways!'

'Please, calm yourself, I beg you. My betrothed is with child,' Winslow urged, wedging himself protectively between Grace and the old woman's jabbing finger.

'I don't care if she's in labour!'

The door to Lord and Lady Farthingdale's cabin promptly slammed shut straight into the couple's bewildered faces.

'This is going to prove more challenging than I thought,' Grace said, somewhat shell-shocked by the experience.

Winslow took his wife-to-be by the hand and hurried to the next cabin. 'Fear not, my love, not all the passengers will be of Lady Farthingdale's disposition. At least I pray not.' Just to be on the safe side, Winslow made the sign of the cross before knocking.

Bang! Bang! Bang!

Promptly, the door opened, revealing a man suited and booted and ready for action despite the late hour. Atop his head sat a jet-black ten-gallon hat, and upon his face bristled a well-presented salt and pepper moustache that curled like the horns of a bull.

Finding himself in the presence of a lady, the man swept the hat from his head and bowed courteously. 'Good evening, madame,' he said before restoring the cowboy hat to his slick black hair. By the man's accent, he originated from one of America's southern states. 'Colonel Darcey at your service. And you are?'

'Grace and Winslow Selsby. At least we will be if we ever get off this damn ship,' Winslow answered.

'Congratulations… I think. Now tell me, Mr and Mrs Selsby to be, why have the engines stopped?'

In place of rudeness and hostility bordering on assault, the couple's explanation was, this time, met with calm acceptance and a pledge to help. Because of Colonel Darcey's military background, he immediately grasped the situation, and before Grace and Winslow knew it, he was thumping on doors one after the other. Soon the three of them were ushering passengers along the corridors and up the stairs. 'Quickly now, ladies and gentlemen,' Colonel Darcey encouraged. 'Up on deck, please.'

Most stumbled into the cold night wearing nothing but bedclothes and slippers beneath their overcoats. They were met with icy air and a dreadful high-pitched howl screaming from Titanic's giant funnels.

'Why are we out here?' they demanded.

'This is nonsense!' they stated.

'A safety drill at midnight is downright unacceptable!' they moaned.

And why would they think anything different? After all, Titanic was the grandest ocean liner ever built. The very notion she might sink was as ludicrous as walking on the moon.

'This is preposterous,' they grumbled, wrapping their arms around their shivering bodies and stamping their frozen feet. 'We'll catch our deaths out here!'

'God willing, you can make your complaints in the morning,' Colonel Darcey said. 'But for now, kindly follow Miss Grace to the nearest lifeboat.' Cajoled by the colonel's persuasive Texan drool, the passengers ambled into Grace's care as obediently as cattle herded across a Kentucky range. 'Much obliged. That's it. Keep rolling.'

'Women and children first,' a White Star Line officer announced. Assisting him, two young crewmen organised the evacuees into the boats. An orderly queue had formed, coiling like a snake around the deck. Even though those waiting in line to disembark believed nothing was amiss, it seemed as if a sombre cloud had descended to affect the mood. Standing tall and proud, husbands and fathers watched the boats slowly lowered into the black waters, smiling reassuringly at their

loved ones until they disappeared into the darkness. However, inside, they couldn't seem to subdue the unsettling sense of foreboding that crawled up the length of their spines like a thousand tiny spiders. 'You'll be fine,' they called. 'We'll be along shortly.'

Winslow escorted a second group of passengers toward the boats. 'Wait your turn, please, gentlemen,' he said, trying to keep a pair of queue hoppers in line.

'It's us, Winnie,' one of the men said. 'Bertie and Titch.'

'Blimey, so it is!'

'Rum do, Winnie. Is the big gal really going under?' Bertie was tall, lean, and appeared perpetually aloof.

'So it would seem, Bertie,' Winslow replied. Still wearing their evening best, it looked like his two friends had come straight from playing cards in the smoking room. He wondered where Fudger was. *The fool's probably passed out at the bar again.* Fudger had an unhealthy liking for brandy. 'Where are your better halves?'

Bertie rolled his eyes. 'They're making themselves look presentable. You know what women are like. They would sooner go down with the ship than be seen without wearing makeup or a posh frock.'

Titch chortled. 'Too right, Bertie.' Titch, as his nickname implied, was short in stature. However, he was more than compensated for what he lacked in inches by the size of his mouth. 'We scouted ahead to secure a berth,' he bellowed. 'Any chance you can bump us up the line, old boy?'

Winslow shook his head. 'I'm afraid not, chaps. In any case, it's women and children only.'

Titch sneered. 'When did you join the crew?'

Winslow didn't much like Titch's tone. 'Just doing my bit to help, that's all.'

Bertie snorted. 'Women and children first… poppycock! We're first-class, Winslow.' He glanced at the other passengers waiting in the queue. 'Most of this lot are second at best.'

'I'm sorry, but those are the captain's orders.' Winslow found himself wondering why he called these men his friends. 'Best of British luck to you both,' he said with indifference, and turning his back on them, he strode away to find his fiancée.

Grace was helping a young girl and her mother into a boat when Winslow caught up with her. 'You know, you ought to be joining them,' he said. Winslow didn't need to explain further. It was obvious he was thinking of the baby.

Grace sighed. 'I know,' she said. 'And I will… soon. I promise. I'll just help another boat or two.'

Winslow squeezed her hands. 'Don't wait too long.'

A disturbance amongst the crowds drew the couple's attention. It was impossible to tell what was happening above the screeching steam bursting from the ship's funnels, but whatever it was, it was causing quite the scene. Deciding to investigate, Grace and Winslow jostled between the queues and headed onto the promenade.

Dozens of passengers were bent over the rails staring below. However, before Grace and Winslow could find out what all the fuss was about, Monroe rushed out on deck. 'I need volunteers,' he yelled. 'There are passengers trapped in steerage. Without help, they'll drown.'

Colonel Darcey volunteered at once.

'I'll go, too,' Winslow said.

Grace grabbed his arm. 'Be careful,' she whispered, holding him tight.

'And you.'

The Beast Cometh

'There's something in the water!'

'Where?'

Frank pointed to a vast shadow rising from the tranquil star-studded sea. 'Dead ahead… No, wait, it's moving. See, now it's floating port side.'

Stan peered into the night but try as he might, he couldn't decipher what *it* was. It looked like nothing more than a giant black hump in the ocean. 'Another iceberg?'

Swivelling in the crow's nest, Frank trailed the thing's movements as it drifted slowly alongside the ship. Not taking his eyes off the anomaly, he grasped the telephone and called the bridge.

'What now?' demanded the flustered voice on the other end of the line.

Yet as Frank and Stan watched, the mysterious object vanished. 'Erm… Nothing, sir. A trick of the light, that's all. My apologies.'

'No apology necessary, Mr Nee,' the bridge officer replied. 'In truth, gentlemen, we are in the lap of the gods and at the mercy of the Atlantic current. We no longer have the means to manoeuvre, and forewarning of any further catastrophes would be most welcome.'

Deep within the flooded depths of Titanic's bowels, angel light flared, a dazzling glare to brighten the darkest shadows. Cassius fused a buckled chunk of metal into position before allowing the swirling current to carry him toward the next hole in Titanic's breached hull. As with the previous openings, the angel began heating the twisted steel. Only once it was glowing red and hissing and spitting in the water was Cassius able to manipulate the ruptured section to his will.

Suddenly the ship lurched. Dislodged, Cassius spiralled head over heels through the turbulent currents churning inside the boiler room. Submerged beneath the water, the angel heard the vessel groan and, more worryingly, the high-pitched shriek of a sea titan.

'Karnakoor,' Cassius hissed. *The monster has returned. Damn Manakel and his useless fish.* How the angel had contrived to cock-up such a simple task was beyond him. *Thanks to me, the hard work was done for him. All he was required to do was finish the fat lump.* Cassius could never forgive the part Manakel played in his fall from grace. *Never was there an angel more villainous.*

The possibility of Manakel's corpse littering the seabed was small consolation when now it seemed he must forsake his post to slay the kraken himself and, in doing so, knowingly condemn the ship and all those aboard to a watery grave.

Cursing Manakel's failures, Cassius abandoned his task and blasted straight through the hull. Launching himself from the stricken ship, he sought the demon before it tore the vessel apart. *All that work for nothing. Manakel has cost Titanic dear. The fool only sent me here out of spite. He wanted the glory of killing Karnakoor for himself.*

Subduing his angel light and rising anger, Cassius propelled himself through the water, sweeping alongside the gigantic liner until he neared the vessel's stern. Diving deeper, he swam beneath, passing the ship's huge motionless propeller blades. Above him, the keel creaked and moaned, the sounds of a dying giant. Hiding below the vessel's enormous mass, Cassius waited.

Within moments, a surge of water buffeted the angel, slamming him upwards against the cold metal of Titanic's hull. The ship rocked from the rising swell, and for a brief time, its propellers turned as seawater was forced through them.

Pushing away from the vessel, Cassius peered into the deep dark Atlantic. An immense shape loomed beneath him, a black shadow, darker even than the fathomless depths of the ocean. The shape ascended, and Cassius saw giant red eyes glowing hungrily in the gloom. The angel's gaze was drawn into their scarlet depths. The more he stared, the further he fell under their power. He was trapped within two burning pools of malevolence, and their roaring flames burned his mind, the pain threatening to destroy him. Yet if he failed, there would be no survivors. Karnakoor's hunger would consume them all. *And I have no wish to end my days inside the belly of something so hideously revolting.*

Defying the beast's hypnotic lure, Cassius summoned his power. Angel light streaked through the murk to blast the demon's baleful eyes. *An eye for an eye…*

At once, the creature's hold over the battle angel shattered. And while Karnakoor's shrieking torment erupted amidst the night-black waters, Cassius' great wings swept him below. The angel headed straight for the monster, arrowing through the sea like a white-hot rocket.

What the…?

After watching her betrothed disappear below with Monroe and Darcey, Grace made her way to the crowds gathering on the promenade. She slipped through the gossiping throng until she was alongside the iron railing. 'What's everybody gawping at?' she asked no one in particular.

'See for yourself,' answered a short, thin man dressed in striped pyjamas and an oversized mackintosh. Like the others, he was staring out to sea and never had Grace seen another soul appear more bewildered than he.

Intrigued, Grace squeezed past him, clambered onto the railings, and peered over the edge. The sky was lit orange by a barrage of flares sent high into the night from Titanic's decks, and as they danced seaward, the odd scene below was highlighted perfectly.

'What do you make of that then, missy?' the man said, shaking his head. 'This night is becoming stranger by the minute.' He rubbed his eyes as if they weren't working.

Grace stared open-mouthed. She couldn't agree with the man more. There were dozens—no, hundreds of dead sharks strewn upon the water's surface, bobbing atop the ocean swell like flotsam. *They're like the great white we found on deck*. And now, just as she'd done earlier, she asked herself how this had come to pass? How had so many sharks succumbed to such a fate?

Without warning, the ship pitched violently. Lost in her thoughts, Grace was caught unawares, and suddenly she was falling headfirst toward the horrible scene.

A hand grabbed her.

'Hold on!' came the short, thin man's voice.

Her heart hammered. She couldn't tear her eyes from the shark-infested waters below her, and even though the creatures were dead, it didn't lessen the fear coursing through her body. Ever so slowly, she felt herself being hauled upwards. More hands grabbed her, and then she was safe. 'Oh my, thank you. Thank you, all!'

The ship remained tilted toward the sea. 'What's happened?' Grace asked, but no one replied. The passengers were distracted by something else. Then screams pierced the night sky.

Staring into the water, the chilling truth was revealed. 'Titanic didn't hit an iceberg,' Grace whispered disbelievingly. She had hit something alive, something enormous, something terrible.

The crowds ran in panic, pushing and shoving to escape. At first, Grace couldn't move. It was as if her limbs had frozen in the chill Atlantic air. Nor could she avert her gaze from the horrifying red eyes blazing like hellfire below the water's surface. Giant oozing tentacles had latched themselves to the ship, and pulling against them, the dreadful thing beneath the waves rose.

Jolted to her senses, Grace scrambled back over the rail. She saw a bolt flash across the sky, much brighter than the falling flares. Then, louder than the steam venting from the funnels above, the monster shrieked. Grace covered her ears, the sound excruciating.

The light shone again, but this time the sea creature smashed it from the sky, and like a shooting star, she watched it streak past her eyes and slam straight into Café Parisian.

The tentacles emerged over the ship's side, bursting over Grace's head. They crashed against the upper decks, pulling and ripping everything in their path to pieces. It was as if the things searched for something. *Or someone*, Grace thought.

Weaving her way past fleeing passengers and ducking under the monster's flailing tentacles, Grace scrambled toward the French-themed café, driven by a need to find out what she saw in the sky.

Above her, terrible cries of anguish sent a shiver of dread lancing through her heart. She glanced upwards. A loud snap echoed in the night and suddenly the crow's nest was falling. Grace gasped as the doomed occupants were snatched into the air and tossed into the beast's cavernous mouth.

Grace pulled her eyes from the awful spectacle and stumbled on. She leapt over a section of the broken crow's nest, and just as another giant tentacle snaked its way across the deck toward her, she crashed through Café Parisian's doors without a moment to spare.

Inside, terrified families huddled together beneath the restaurant's tables. Too frightened to speak, they stared at Grace with wide, startled eyes.

Gathering herself, Grace moved deeper into the café. It didn't take long to spot where the shooting star had crashed landed. Starlight gleamed through a gaping hole in the roof, and below, lying amidst the splintered remains of a ruined dining table, was Captain Cassius.

'I don't understand,' Grace whispered to herself. 'What is *he* doing here?' She glanced up to the hole and then back to the broken table. From what she could ascertain, the captain was precisely where her shooting star ought to be. *It doesn't make any sense.*

Cassius groaned.

'You're alive.' Grace knelt at the man's side. He appeared to be uninjured. In fact, there wasn't a mark on him.

The lights inside the restaurant dimmed and then flickered. Outside, beneath the stars, the monster raged. Abruptly, the ship rolled the opposite way—to port—and so vigorously that Grace and the unconscious Captain Cassius skidded uncontrollably across the restaurant's green-carpeted floor. Their slide was only halted when the pair became wedged between the legs of a dining table. Thankfully, Café Parisian's furniture was well secured. Upturned chairs, broken crockery, and foot-long French baguettes tumbled past them. Somewhere near, a child screamed. Then, during a merciful lull during which the creature's terrifying roaring eased, Grace heard the desperate prayers of the people sheltering beside her.

Grace's innards lurched again, and with a mighty thump, the ship righted herself. 'Oh, thank goodness,' she whispered with relief. However, her fear of being capsized was replaced by her fear of the dark. All at once, the lights blinked out. And not only inside Café Parisian. The entire ship had seemingly lost power. Fresh screams erupted from Titanic's decks, echoing into the night sky, but Grace didn't notice. *Why is Captain Cassius glowing in the dark?*

As Grace and the frightened souls taking refuge inside the restaurant stared, the strange aura radiating from the captain's body intensified until, after a blinding flash, the light receded to a faint golden sheen.

'What the…?' Grace muttered incredulously.

The captain was gone and in his place rose an angel.

'I could murder a brew,' he said.

Grace's face dropped like she'd suffered a stroke. She shared a look of astonishment with the other passengers who, bar none, had crawled from beneath the relative safety of their tabletop shelters to gaze in wonder at the man with wings. 'God be praised!' they said. 'A miracle!' Astonishment was proceeded by incomprehension, and then in Grace's case, incomprehension was followed by irrepressible outrage.

'You stand there shining like the North Star with… with ruddy angel wings… wearing, well, some sort of absurd fancy dress costume demanding, of all things, a damn *cup of tea* while the ship is being ripped to pieces by a hundred-ton octopus?'

Cassius raised an eyebrow. The woman's reaction was unexpected. He immediately decided he liked her. 'Facing a kraken in battle is thirsty work, Grace.' Without further ado, he sauntered into the restaurant's wrecked kitchens, where he began heating a pan of water with his bare hands. 'Now, where do you think they keep the tea?'

Grace stomped after him. 'What are you doing?' she demanded. 'People are dying out there. Can't you hear their screams? I thought angels were supposed to help.'

The water began bubbling in the pan. Cassius bopped down on his haunches. 'Are, there you are.' He scooped up a handful of loose tea leaves from where they lay scattered beside a broken jar. 'Alas, no strainer. Oh, well, needs must.' Shrugging his shoulders, he dumped the leaves into the boiling water and gave them a quick poke with a finger.

Grace was furious. 'You try my patience, sir! The Lord Almighty will hear of your pig-headedness.' Although she wasn't entirely sure how she would convey the message.

Cassius was confused. 'I'm not sure what swine have to do with anything? And regardless of pig heads, a female in your condition really ought to keep calm.'

Grace held her small bump protectively.

'If you must know, and I usually don't make a habit of explaining myself to mortals, the tannin in tea helps me better absorb light,' he said. 'Without it, I won't last another five minutes against our nasty little friend out there.'

Grace really didn't have a clue what he was talking about. 'What light?' Hadn't he noticed it was past midnight and the power had gone off?

'Starlight, of course.' Pinching his nose, the angel lifted the pan to his lips. 'Bottoms up!' Tilting his head back, he gulped down the tea in one go.

'You are peculiar indeed,' Grace said, observing him with a sideways glance. 'Are all angels so strange?'

Cassius picked bits of black leaf from his teeth. 'I'm not sure I like being called *peculiar*.' Actually, he'd been called a damn sight worse but rarely by a human. 'Did you know that some of you, the nicer not-so-stupid ones, are chosen as angels when you die? Think about that before you choose to berate one of my kind in the future.'

It was Grace's turn to look confused. She didn't understand the relevance. Anyway, having to fight sea monsters wasn't a

particularly enticing reason for coming back as an angel. She would much rather go straight to Heaven, thank you very much.

Like moths to a candle, the passengers gathered inside the kitchens. They stared, transfixed by this heavenly visitor sent to protect them in their hour of need. The night's atrocities were forgotten in the angel's presence… but not for long.

An almighty crash exploded behind them. Glass and debris shrieked into the kitchens, showering everyone inside as they fell to their hands and knees in panic.

Coughing dust from her lungs, Grace pushed herself upright. The restaurant was all but gone. A few stubborn tables remained unwilling to free themselves from their bolts and brackets, but everything else had been swept into the ocean.

'Ah, ha! Perfect!' Cassius announced jubilantly. He strode out into the night and flung his arms and wings wide, bathing his body in starlight amidst the shattered wreckage of Café.

Survival

Winslow followed Monroe and Darcey down into the ship. People ambled about in the corridors and on staircases as if they had all the time in the world. Some congregated in the reception rooms, playing cards or chatting amiably with friends, preferring to wait for rescue in the warm.

It beggars belief, Winslow thought as he raced past. He noticed Lord and Lady Farthingdale arguing fiercely with a crewmember. They were demanding the bar be reopened. *At least they've ventured from their cabin.*

There was no sense of urgency at all. Yet the lower the rescue party descended, the less this proved true. Passengers rushed from their berths, desperate to escape the rising water. Some folk stayed behind to help. Winslow saw a kindly gentleman aiding an elderly couple along the corridor. He had linked arms with theirs, and while they shuffled toward the stairs, he urged them on with words of encouragement. 'Remarkable progress! I do believe we have managed a whole twenty yards in the last quarter of an hour, perhaps even a smidgen more!'

Soon Winslow and his companions were splashing through seawater in the lower levels.

'Not much further,' Monroe said.

Up ahead, at the end of a long, straight passageway, Mr Barrett and another man, just as broad and burly as the stoker, were throwing their weight against a metal rod wedged into a door frame.

Winslow stared in horror. On the other side, the corridor was completely flooded. He saw hands hammering against the glass set into the door's centre, desperate to break through. Sometimes a haunted face appeared, their eyes bulging and mouth open in a silent scream. *Poor souls,* Winslow lamented. *They can't have much time left.*

'It's no good,' Barrett declared, his beer barrel chest heaving with exertion. 'The blasted thing won't budge.'

Colonel Darcey joined the men. 'Then let us lend our strength to the cause,' he said, shepherding Winslow and Monroe forward. Together, they heaved on the bar. At first, there was no change, and when the metal rod began to bend, they feared the worst. But then there was a creek, then a moan, and suddenly, the heavy metal door flew from its hinges and with it came the crashing roar of the ocean.

Flinging himself sideways, Winslow glimpsed the door smashing into Barrett and Monroe. An instant later, he was struck by a wall of water, the savage impact knocking the air from his lungs. It felt as if he'd been flattened by a freight train. The raging current tore him from his feet and dashed him headlong down the corridor.

Swirling in the water's depths, Winslow thought he was going to drown. Bodies thumped into him, hands grabbed, feet kicked. For a time, submerged beneath the surface, he tumbled uncontrollably. Unable to breathe, his chest burned. And then he bashed against something hard. Instinctively, Winslow stretched out an arm. His hands grasped cold metal. Curling his numb fingers, he hung on for dear life. The surging water snatched at his body, trying to rip him free and sweep him to his death.

Thank Heaven, a staircase. Gritting his teeth, Winslow began hauling himself upwards. Fighting against the raging water, he climbed the metal steps one by one. Finally, his battered head emerged from the torrent into blessed air, and he gasped for breath. Coughing and spluttering, Winslow inched to safety. Yet as he returned his gaze to the rushing water, he was dismayed by the number of bodies racing past him—men, women, and children.

Winslow reached into the water, groping for an arm or a leg. He seized a flailing limb, but he couldn't hold on. The speed at which the bodies hurtled past made the task impossibly difficult. Despairing, Winslow tried again and again. At last, he hooked a floundering child by an ankle, and this time Winslow reeled his catch home, fishing the young girl from the torrent, half-drowned and shaking with fear.

Winslow held the girl close. 'It's alright. You're safe now,' he soothed. 'Quickly, up the steps. I'm right behind you.'

The ship swayed back and forth, groaning ominously. Gripping the staircase's iron handrail, Winslow and the child began climbing to safety. On the deck above, Winslow was reunited with Colonel Darcey. Not only had the indomitable Texan survived the terrors below, but he'd somehow rescued a dozen souls from the floods. Yet there was no sign of Barrett or Monroe. Lighting their way with torchlight, they clambered up the Grand Staircase toward salvation with hope burning in their hearts.

'Come on,' Winslow encouraged. 'By Jove, we're all but there!'

'Do as the man says, and we'll be in the lifeboats before you can whistle Yankee Doodle,' Darcey added, bringing up the rear and keeping up the spirits.

Other stragglers joined them en route. Many had lost loved ones to the hazardous lower levels. It was a sombre procession, and all those ambling onwards had come to realise Titanic's grim fate—she was sinking, and if they couldn't escape her decks before she went under, they never would.

However, there was something they didn't understand. What was happening up top? The further they rose, the clearer the sounds of chaos became. Winslow could only guess the passengers were rioting. Perhaps they fought amongst themselves for the right to claim a boat? It was unthinkable. But in matters of life and death, who truly knew how they would react in such a situation?

Mounting the Grand Staircase's final flight of stairs, the way was brightened by a host of gleaming stars shining through the glass dome above their heads. Yet when Winslow gazed upwards toward their beauty, he saw to his disbelief that the dome was gone.

What has caused such a thing? He struggled to think of anything that might have led to the dome's destruction. Perhaps a funnel had fallen? He prayed Grace was safe. Whatever was responsible, Winslow was left unnerved by the oddity, and it was with trepidation, not hope, that he led the survivors crunching up the stairs through the broken glass and out on deck.

'Sweet mother of God,' Colonel Darcey whispered. 'What fresh hell is this?'

Titanic's power had returned. Yet its restoration was nothing more than a curse because the nightmare unfolding before them was now visible in all its horrifying glory.

'Heaven protect us.'

The scene was a warzone in all but name. Titanic's decks were devasted. The crow's nest, the restaurants, the lounges, the stately cabins, and even the bridge itself all smashed to ruin, and their remnants scattered like refuse. The ship's enormous funnels shrieked above the screams, a terrible cacophony accompanying the passenger's looming demise.

However, it was the monstrous instigator of this wanton destruction and the demon's celestial combatant that demanded their attention: a giant sea monster from the darkest depths of the ocean and a golden angel brighter than the stars.

'Hell lays claim to our souls, but Heaven fights to save us! Can we trust our eyes, sir?' Winslow asked Darcey.

'By all things holy, what chance is there against such a foe, even for an angel?'

Winslow found the colonel's words hard to deny. *A battle between Heaven and Hell, and we're stuck in the middle*. He sighed lamentably. *Rotten luck*.

Wherever Winslow looked, he saw panic. A madness swept through the ship affecting both body and mind. Rather than face the demon, passengers flung themselves at the mercy of the sea. Others, accepting their destiny, sunk to their knees to wait for the end. Those with any sense chose to flee, either below deck into Titanic's flooding heart or to the stern of the ship, the place furthest from the monster's reach.

The little girl held in Winslow's arms began whimpering once more. 'It's alright, little one,' he whispered softly. 'I'll not let you go. I promise.' He eyed the devastation surrounding them with hopelessness. To survive this hell, they needed to escape, and the only way to do that was by boat.

Time was running out. Winslow prayed Grace had already secured passage and was far away from Titanic and her horrors. If the Atlantic Ocean pouring through the vessel's hull didn't sink her, the giant octopus undoubtedly would.

Winslow watched as the hellish monstrosity's many appendages snaked into the sky, desperate to smash the angel to his death. Lancing beams of light shot from the angel's hands, striking the monster's flesh, but the bombardment seemed only to enrage the creature further.

Perhaps the angel's efforts are not in vain, Winslow mused. If nothing else, the beast was distracted. *Distracted enough for us to slip past unnoticed?*

Titan Fall

'Come, we can't stay here,' Grace said. 'We should find somewhere safer—if there is such a place—and pray the angel prevails against the demon.'

To be honest, she didn't hold much hope for either scenario, especially not the latter. From what she'd seen, she guessed the angel wasn't among Heaven's elite. *All mouth and no trousers.* Grace had encountered men cut from the same cloth before.

Creeping from the restaurant's kitchens, Grace gauged their chances. If they didn't move soon, they would be flattened. The kraken had hauled its enormous, bloated frame high out of the water. Its grotesque head now slumped atop A-Deck like a beached whale, and its relentless tentacles thrashed skyward in search of Cassius.

To his credit and Grace's surprise, the angel was putting on rather a good show. At least in terms of entertainment. *I'll book him for the wedding*, Grace mused, peering up into the night. *The guests will adore him. Who needs fireworks when you've an angel?* She had the unsettling feeling that she was becoming hysterical. *By God, but he's infectious... and brave. Yes,* very *brave.* Perhaps she had been too hard on him. *Actions speak louder than words.* And oh boy, were his actions screaming. It really was quite astonishing what a cup of tea could do.

Clambering through the wreckage, Grace headed for the rear of the vessel. It appeared higher than before, and as she and the passengers from the café dashed past flying debris and groping tentacles, it felt as if they were running uphill through a battlefield. Nearing the Poop Deck, where hundreds of survivors had assembled to await the end, she could hear a jolly tune competing with the ship's groaning and the monster's shrieking. In the face of certain death, Titanic's band played on.

Having negotiated the beast, Winslow and the survivors reached the Boat Deck unscathed. However, in place of hope, they only found more misery.

The ship's prow now dipped well below the waves, and the seawater surged ever higher. As for the lifeboats themselves, they were nowhere to be seen, as was true of Grace. It was difficult not to admit defeat and submit to the inevitability of death.

Winslow was tempted to join those who, realising their doom, had crumpled to the sodden deck awaiting the ocean to claim their broken souls. But he couldn't give up. What if Grace hadn't fled in a lifeboat but was still aboard Titanic? And what of the frightened little girl wrapped in his arms? Surely, she was worth fighting for?

'Our best chance is to get ourselves to the ship's stern,' Winslow announced. 'Who's with me?'

Most ignored him, preferring to let the sea wash them away, but a few ambled forward in hope, including Colonel Darcey. 'I'm with you, Selsby,' he said, tipping his cowboy hat.

'And so am I,' Monroe added. The White Star Line officer appeared from what was left of the bridge cradling a sizeable trunk in his arms. 'At least I am as far as the demon.' He dumped the box into the rising water and broke open the lid.

Inside was an assortment of pistols and flare guns. 'Compliments of the Captain,' he said.

Titanic's captain was resolved to remain on the ruined bridge, come what may. Winslow admired the man's sense of duty. A captain should always be the last to abandon his ship. 'Did you see what happened to Mr Barrett?' Monroe had escaped the lower levels, and perhaps so had the chief stoker.

Monroe shook his head.

Winslow thought as much. 'I say, what are you going to do with that lot?' he asked, nodding his head at the assortment of goodies stacked inside the trunk.

Monroe offered Winslow a pistol. 'I'm going to help the angel,' he declared. 'After all, it's my duty as an officer to defend my ship, is it not? Even if it is against a sea monster.'

Winslow declined the weapon. 'If it's all the same with you, I would rather live a teeny bit longer.' Winslow suspected Monroe's heroics were nothing more than a suicide mission. 'I have a little girl to protect and a fiancée to find.'

Darcey took the pistol instead, then equipped himself with a flare gun for good measure. He grinned at Monroe. 'I never could resist hunting big game.'

Scrambling onto Winslow's back, the little girl repositioned in readiness for the ordeal ahead. Holding on tight, she wrapped her arms and legs around him. It was time to run the gauntlet.

Winslow splashed away through the surging water, leaving those resigned to their fate behind. Beside him, stern-faced and ready to do battle, strode Darcey and Monroe, and behind them, half a dozen diehard passengers praying for a miracle.

Descending the stairs from the Boat Deck to the promenade, they quickly found themselves wading through deeper water. Titanic's prow was sinking fast, and as they struggled from the Atlantic's swirling clutches, the great ship shivered ominously. Titanic began to capitulate, surrendering to the endless ocean and Karnakoor's insatiable hunger. Those aboard knew it was only a matter of time before she was dragged kicking and screaming to the seabed.

Emerging from the waters onto dry decking, Winslow ran. The stern rose as the prow sank, the incline ahead increasing by the second. Above, angel light flashed. Yet regardless of Cassius' efforts, the ravenous demon continued to feast upon the living, scooping them up in its giant tentacles before hurling them into its gaping maw. As Winslow approached the creature, he could not think how they would pass unnoticed when all who tried failed.

'Winnie, is that you down there?'

Winslow skidded to a halt. *I know that voice.* He craned his head skyward, and there, suckered to a tentacle directly above him, was Bertie.

'Ahoy, Winslow!' And there was Titch, snared in the grasp of another writhing appendage beside his friend.

'Hello below!' And Fudger, too.

'Rotten luck, chaps,' Winslow called back, not really knowing what to say.

'Yes, well, I suppose it can't be helped, old bean. We'll have to reschedule the cricket match… indefinitely.'

Winslow opened his mouth to reply but couldn't think of a damn thing to say. The absurdity of the moment left him tongue-tied.

'Good luck with the wedding, Winnie,' Fudger called. 'Here, have a drink on me.' A handful of notes began fluttering down from the night sky.

'Where are your better halves?' Winslow finally managed. *Fingers crossed they haven't already been eaten.*

'All safe and sound on the–'

And that was the last Winslow heard from his friends. *Well, at least their good ladies escaped their husbands' awful fate. Rest in peace, chaps.*

Aiming for the demon's glowing red eyes, Darcey and Monroe blasted the kraken with their flares and pistols, hoping to blind the monster or, at the very least, distract it long enough for Winslow to safely cross its path.

'A direct hit!' Monroe hollered. 'Now go!'

'God's speed, Winslow!' Darcey cried.

Winslow ran. The beast's writhing tentacles thrashed wildly, pounding against the deck. A deep hole yawned open in front of him. It was too late to do anything else but leap. Sailing through the air, he prayed he had jumped high enough. A second later, he thumped down on the other side. Stumbling, he fell to his knees. *Blimey, that was too close.*

Gathering himself, he sped on. He felt the little girl panting, her hot breath blowing on the skin of his neck. A tentacle flashed toward him. Somehow, he ducked beneath the swooping appendage. Straightening, he powered forward. The ship's stern rose before him. He could see people ahead, packed together like sardines. He could hear their screams, too, desperate and fearful. If he was going to die, he was determined to die hand in hand with his betrothed.

From under Winslow's feet, the muffled thudding of exploding boilers rumbled from deep within the stricken vessel. As the shrieking steam bellowing from Titanic's funnels ceased, a succession of fiery eruptions blasted through the deck. Winslow swerved his way between gushes of deadly flame spewing fifty feet into the sky. It was like crossing a detonating minefield. Titanic's tormented structure shuddered as she struggled to stay afloat under the immense stresses assailing her vast bulk.

Winslow was so close. The passengers ahead urged him on. He could see them waving their hands and arms, even their hats in the air, beckoning him toward them. Winslow glanced left and right. He was alone. *I'm the last.* Behind him, gunshots rang into the night. *Darcey and Monroe's last stand.* And then he saw her, the most wondrous sight in all of creation, a picture to rekindle his lost hope and banish the nightmares stalking his soul… he saw his Grace.

Grace's beaming smile pulled Winslow toward her as if he were a vessel lost at sea, and she the bright torch of a lighthouse, a beacon guiding him to safety. A final flight of stairs stood between him and his betrothed. He scrambled upwards on hands and knees, the staircase now a near-vertical climb. Each step gained felt like a mountain conquered. Deckchairs, musical instruments, small children, and anything that wasn't secured flew at him, threatening to dislodge him and send him and his passenger into the waiting abyss behind. He hauled himself and the little girl higher and higher until, at last, and thanks to Heaven, he reached the final step. Yet as he mounted that last tread, he felt something coil around his legs.

In that awful moment, Winslow knew he wasn't going to make it. He was done for. Acting quickly, he pulled the little girl from his back and hurled her into Grace's waiting hands. 'Toodle-pip, darling!' Jerked from the staircase, he was carried high into the darkness.

Grace's smile faded, and her face crumpled. She couldn't watch. Together, she and the little girl sobbed into each other's arms. Winslow was gone.

Through the souls of her feet, Grace felt Titanic shudder. Swiftly, the sensation was followed by a great noise, a deafening roar rising from deep below. The angle of the sinking ship increased sharply. Grace fought her way through the desperate masses, shoving past bodies to claim a place at the vessel's rear. No sooner had her numb fingers grasped the cold metal railings circling the ship's perimeter did Titanic's lights fail, first a flicker, then darkness. As screams filled the night, she felt the ship's stern rise again, becoming a sheer drop. The little girl clung so tightly that her fingernails drew blood from Grace's neck.

In her final moments, a strange calmness washed through Grace, an acceptance of her fate. Cassius dived and weaved in the night sky among the gleaming stars above. There was something magical about the sight, something that touched her soul to the very core.

The cries and screams quietened, and a deathly hush descended over the ship and her passengers. The survivors clung to Titanic and to their final seconds on this earth. Nonetheless, in their moment of ruin, they stared into the night not with despair filling their hearts but reverence. Erupting from the black sea rose figures of gleaming gold and borne upon majestic wings, they soared high above the doomed ship.

Uniting with Cassius, Manakel, Zadkiel, Sachael, and Neos shot arcing beams of light into the night. Yet this time, they didn't aim their power directly at the demon but at the closest of Titanic's colossal funnels. The metal throbbed red, then a searing white. And as the super-heated cylinder fell, the angels drove the enormous shaft at the kraken, thrusting the makeshift weapon like a giant red-hot harpoon deep into the sea demon's cavernous maw.

Writhing in agony, Karnakoor's tentacles thrashed against Titanic's ravaged decks. Another dreadful groan rumbled from the ship's insides, proceeded at once by a repetitive booming. Then, with a final sudden roar, Titanic split in two. The vessel's prow vanished beneath the ocean, and with it sank the vast corpse of Karnakoor, the last of the sea titans.

'Don't look,' Grace whispered into the little girl's ear. Grace had climbed over the railings, and now she held on facing the onrushing blackness of the Atlantic. All around them, passengers fell screaming to their deaths. 'Take a deep breath,' she said. Then, as the remnants of Titanic surged beneath the surface, they were gone.

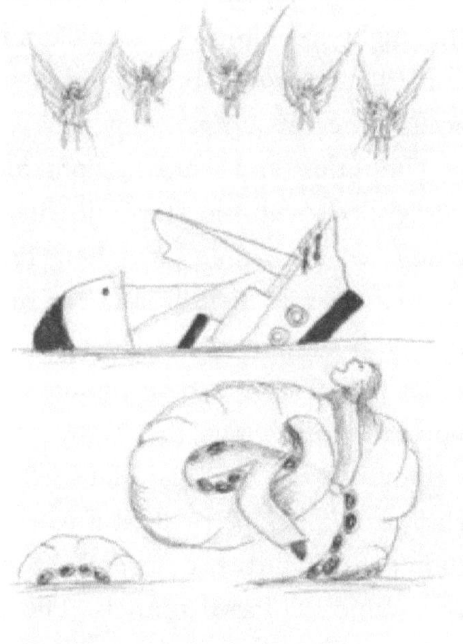

Grace let go of the railings as they entered the water, but she and the little girl were sucked deep down in the dying ship's wake, the thundering of the ocean filling their ears.

They swirled amidst the freezing depths, the shocking cold threatening to stop their hearts dead. For a time, they floated in the void, clinging together, awaiting the end. Yet in the far distance, brightening the impenetrable shadow, there was a light, a golden light. And as it glided nearer, Grace felt her hope resurrected. Cassius was coming for them.

~ The End ~

Demon Hunters

The Chronicles of Cassius

~ Volgamare ~

Vietnam, 1965

When Randy Hudson's platoon finds themselves lost amidst the Ia Drang Valley, things begin to turn weird. A strange encounter with a big marine and a North Vietnamese patrol results in a remarkable truce and a desperate fight for survival. The two enemies must unite against a common threat or risk a fate worse than death.

Cassius and his unlikely coalition must seek and destroy the festering evil at the heart of the jungle before all hell breaks loose.

Demon Hunters

Heroic Fantasy through the Ages

Dog Tags

'Down!' Staff Sergeant Jerry Powell cried.

Ahead, gunfire screamed from the jungle. The treeline flared with flashing muzzles, and the air exploded with shrieking red-hot lead. The men of 2nd Platoon hit the ground hard and fast, submerging themselves in the tall grass covering the clearing.

'Marshal's hit!' a desperate voice called somewhere near.

Pushing his face into the dirt, Private Randy Hudson gripped his rifle with fingers and palms slick with sweat. Squeezing his eyes shut, he eased a shaking hand from his M16 and fumbled beneath his shirt. *Where is the damn thing?* Taking a calming breath, he felt for the chain secured around his neck, feeding its length through his fingers until finally pulling the small silver cross free. Curling his hand around the crucifix, he grasped it tight. 'Jo's a good man, Lord. See him right,' he whispered. A prayer, not for himself but for Private Joseph Marshal.

Bullets hissed through the grass above Private Hudson's head. 'Make no mistake, we're pinned down good and proper,' the soldier muttered grimly.

Coms were down, and the platoon's route to the extraction zone and a ride back to base was swarming with the North Vietnamese Army's finest regiment, the 66th. 2nd Platoon's commander, Lieutenant Richard Perry—otherwise known as *Dick* but never to his face—had led them stumbling from one NVA patrol to another. It was a wonder any of them were still breathing. Then, attempting to circumnavigate the enemy, the lieutenant got them lost somewhere in the Ia Drang Valley or, as the grunts liked to call the nightmarish place, *Death Valley.*

'On my mark, 2nd Platoon will advance on the enemy's position!'

Hudson despaired. *Another attempt at getting us all killed.* Lieutenant Perry's leadership wasn't held in the highest regard by his men, and neither was he.

'Call an airstrike, sir,' Specialist Curtis 'Big Bird' Goose hollered. Big Bird was six and a half feet tall and carried the platoon's M60 machine gun, the pig—named after the weapon's insatiable appetite for ammunition.

'The radio is inoperable, Goose,' Sergeant Griffin replied away to Private Hudson's right.

Hudson rolled onto his back and stared into the blue. NVA gunfire continued to rattle across the clearing. He was sure he could see the air shimmer as the bullets whistled above him. *We'd all be dead if it weren't for the grass.* The chest-high elephant grass was a godsend. 'Can't we crawl back the way we came?' It was worth a shout, but Hudson didn't hold much hope of changing the lieutenant's mind.

'There's no other way,' Lieutenant Perry called. 'We have no choice but to engage.'

I thought he'd say that. Hudson yanked out his silver cross again, and this time he began praying for himself.

'Screw this!' Big Bird unslung his M60, and with Private 'Jacko' Jackson at his side—Goose's assistant gunner, whose task it was to feed Big Bird's ravenous pig with ammo—the two of them burst from cover.

'Get down, Goose!' Hudson heard someone shout. But Big Bird and Jacko were on the rampage, and neither Heaven nor Hell was going to stop them.

Bellowing at the top of their lungs, Goose and Jackson bulldozed through the grass, heading straight for the enemy. Rounds screamed at them, tugging at their uniforms and churning up the ground at their feet. Living a charmed life, the pair mounted the broad trunk of a fallen banyan tree fifty yards from the NVA's position.

'Eat my pig!' Big Bird hollered. The M60 roared into life, blasting the bush ahead until everything along the treeline was shredded into wood chippings.

Seizing their chance, the platoon pushed to their feet. 'Go, go, go!' Staff Sergeant Powell yelled.

The soldiers charged the enemy's position, storming past the M60 crew atop the fallen tree trunk. As Hudson ploughed headlong through the grass, he fired his M16 aimlessly into the jungle. Then he and his brothers-in-arms were among the trees, and the NVA were running… but not before a final burst from an Ak-47 caught Goose, toppling him from his perch.

Big Bird was down.

'Secure the area,' Lieutenant Perry commanded. 'Charlie is still out there.' Charlie was what the US soldiers called the enemy. The lieutenant's eyes didn't stop scanning the jungle for their return. The NVA were tenacious and cunning, and rarely did they concede defeat after a firefight.

'What about Marshal and Goose?' Private Hudson demanded. He could see Jacko through the trees, still sitting on the tree trunk in the clearing.

'First, secure the position, then go with Private Grant and help Jackson bring in the injured.'

Private Hudson nodded. Although by the look of Jacko, who slumped dejectedly with his head in his hands, it was too late for Goose. *Not Big Bird, too*, Hudson despaired. The soldier had seemed invincible to Randy, but now he feared he was gone like so many others. 2nd Platoon had lost some good men over the past twenty-four hours.

A single shot echoed ominously through the clearing, jerking the Private from his thoughts. Hudson swung toward the sound and saw Jackson fall sideways from the banyan trunk. In the next instance, 2nd Platoon's guns opened fire.

'Contact!' Staff Sergeant Powell cried, blasting a North Vietnamese soldier armed with a Soviet-built semi-automatic through the heart. A second enemy force emerged screaming from the elephant grass. US riflemen picked their targets, skillfully dropping the NVA soldiers before they made the treeline.

'Quickly, into the jungle,' Lieutenant Perry ordered breathlessly.

'What about our fallen?' Private Hudson questioned. Leaving a man behind, dead or alive, was not something a soldier felt happy about. To be buried on home soil was the least they and their families deserved.

'We have no choice, Private Hudson. You'll die beside them if you go back out there.'

Hudson didn't like it, but Lieutenant Perry was right this time. To go back now was suicide.

The platoon delved deeper into the jungle. In places, the terrain was so dense the soldiers needed to hack their way through the undergrowth with their knives.

'Dick doesn't know where we're going, does he?' Private Grant said, slashing a vine from his path. Larry Grant was a

straight talker from Ohio. He told it how it was, no messing.

'He never has, so why start now?'

Randy Hudson and Larry Grant were as thick as thieves. They went to school together, enlisted together, and now they fought in the godforsaken jungle together.

'We should have gone back for Big Bird and Jacko,' Hudson said. The thought of leaving them behind was gnawing at his innards.

'Don't forget Jo. He was a good man.'

'Yeah, Jo, too,' Hudson said.

'Do you know what upsets me the most?'

Hudson shook his head.

'Now Charlie's got another M60 to kill us with.'

The M60 was the US Army's heavy machine gun, capable of inflicting serious pain. Losing the weapon to the enemy left a bitter taste in the mouth.

The longer the morning wore on and the further from their dead comrades they marched, the more agitated Hudson became. 'I'm going back for them,' he finally announced to his friend, ducking under a sprawling branch.

'What? For Goose and Jackson?'

'Yeah, and Marshal.'

'And how the hell are you going to do that? Do you know how much Big Bird weighs? I'll tell you, shall I? As much as an M48. And I'm guessing the other two aren't gonna be a whole lot lighter.' The M48 Patton was the US army's battle tank.

'I can bring back their dog tags,' Hudson argued. 'At least their families will have something to remember them by.' He'd already helped retrieve a dozen after the firefight at the drop zone. He knew the mission was destined to be a nightmare after such a terrible start.

'You're nuts, Randy. If you don't get killed, you'll get court-martialled.'

'Dick wouldn't dare.'

'True. The man's got less backbone than one of these damn jungle snakes.' Grant shook his head. 'Hell, Randy. You know I can't let you go alone, don't you?'

Hudson grinned. 'I hoped you'd say that.'

By midday, the platoon had lost the enemy and themselves. The weather, as ever, was sweltering, an unrelenting oppressive heat to sap the strength and disorientate the mind.

Lieutenant Perry ordered a brief halt to take on food and fluids—and secretly to gauge his bearings. The lieutenant wouldn't admit his incompetence in front of the men, but as usual, he hadn't a clue where they were.

'Now's our chance,' Hudson whispered. Lieutenant Perry was hunkered beside Sergeant Griffin. The pair were trying to make the sergeant's radio work. The rest of the twenty-five-strong platoon were slumped amongst the trees trying to grab five minutes of shut-eye. 'Are you with me?'

Grant eyed his comrades thoughtfully, ensuring Lieutenant Perry and the other men were sufficiently distracted. Grant nodded. 'I can't believe we're doing this.'

Staff Sergeant Powell, the only reason Lieutenant Perry hadn't managed to get everyone killed, was organising sentries to watch for the NVA while the men rested. And as Private Hudson and Private Grant snuck away into the undergrowth, they exchanged a knowing wink with Private Hicks, who Powell had chosen for guard duty. Hicks was sound. He wouldn't give them away.

It wasn't difficult for Hudson and Grant to retrace their steps. Twenty-five soldiers running for their lives leave a trail a blind man can track. So far, there was no sign of the enemy. Nonetheless, there were other things to worry about besides the NVA or Viet Cong. The surrounding vegetation was teeming with life, and like the North Vietnamese, most of it didn't want the United States military stomping through their land. The jungle was home to vast nests of stinging weaver ants, deadly centipedes as long as a man's arm, venomous vipers and pythons, not to mention spiders, bears, leopards, and giant buffalos that liked nothing more than charging at unsuspecting

Americans. And when the wildlife wasn't trying to kill you, the flora and fauna were, strangling vines, poisonous Flame Lilies, and deadly Heartbreak Glass were just a few examples to avoid. It wasn't like the park back home. This playground was lethal.

'Did you hear what happened to Captain Banks?' Grant whispered, and he didn't wait for an answer. 'Dragged from the mess tent by a damn tiger!'

'What a way to go.'

'There are worse ways, Randy.'

To be honest, Hudson couldn't think of many except for walking into one of the enemy's booby traps. Mines, tripwires, and pits were among their favourites. The NVA and Viet Cong excelled in creating imaginative ways to inflict pain on their foes, and getting captured could be even worse. A visit to Hoa Lo prison—or the 'Hanoi Hilton' as the POWs called the hellhole jail—was best given a wide berth. Highlights included regular beatings, solitary confinement, complementary manacles, and a menu consisting of nothing but watery soup lovingly mixed with the guard's bodily waste. Not forgetting an extensive list of gruesome tortures like being tied and hung from meat hooks, whipped with razor-sharp bamboo, and strapped to beds for days on end with flesh-eating rats for company.

Creeping through the jungle with their fingers primed on the triggers of their M16 rifles, the two grunts eventually made it back to the scene of the firefight. Beyond the treeline, swathed in elephant grass, was the clearing. And there, twisted and gnarled like a decaying shipwreck half-submerged in a sea of brown and green, was the fallen banyan tree.

Here the jungle bore the scars of battle. Trunks were split, bark stripped, plants lacerated, and foliage decimated. All evidence of the damage caused by an M60 machine gun.

'Where are the bodies?' Hudson murmured.

The enemy dead were gone. The two soldiers peered from the undergrowth with trepidation. Were the NVA out there waiting for them? For what felt like an age, they stood and stared, searching the tall swaying grass over and over. Finally, convinced the area was safe, Grant nodded at the clearing. The pair abandoned the cover offered by the jungle and began wading through the elephant grass.

Grant clambered on top of the fallen tree, and with M16 raised, he kept watch while Hudson manoeuvred around the ancient banyan, its rotting branches like the limbs of a toppled giant, stretching far and wide.

Hudson's heart sank. Big Bird and Jacko were nowhere to be seen. *The NVA must have taken them.* It was no surprise to find the M60 missing too. Hudson re-emerged on the other side of the tree, shaking his head.

Grant shrugged his shoulders as if to say, 'well, that's that then.' There was nothing else they could do. Then Hudson pointed his gun deeper into the clearing.

Grant rolled his eyes. They'd got lucky so far, and if Goose and Jackson were gone, surely so was Marshal. But before he could talk his friend out of doing anything rash, Hudson had disappeared.

'Randy,' Grant hissed. 'We need to go!' Crouched low on the banyan tree, he spotted Hudson ploughing further into the sea of grass. Grant stared through the sights of his M16, diligently scanning the surrounding landscape for hostiles. He performed a complete 360 before clocking his friend again.

Abruptly, Hudson halted, and then an instant later, he vanished into the elephant grass. *Looks like he's found Jo*, Grant mused, blinking sweat from his eyes. He waited impatiently for his friend to resurface. 'What are you doing, Randy?' he muttered. *How long does it take to remove a man's dog tag?*

Suddenly, ten yards from his previous position, Hudson's helmeted head popped up from the grass… and then he was gone again. 'What the—' A burst of gunfire crackled through the clearing. Hudson was visible once more and pounding through the grass straight at Grant. There was someone chasing him.

Once Hudson was beyond the fallen tree, Grant squeezed the trigger of his M16. The assault rifle spewed a deluge of rounds into the onrushing enemy soldier, sweeping him from his feet.

Except it wasn't an enemy soldier.

Grant lowered his smoking weapon with shaking hands. *Oh my God, what have I done? I've shot one of our own.* He'd recognised the uniform too late.

A low moan issued from somewhere amidst the tall grass.

'Thank Christ, he's still alive!' *But how can anyone survive a dozen rounds to the chest?*

'Run, Larry!' Hudson cried. 'Run for your life!'

The Dead of Night

'I fired and fired, and still he wouldn't go down,' Private Randy Hudson explained. The young man's eyes couldn't stop searching the vegetation for signs of movement. He didn't dare blink. What if Marshal was still out there?

'How?' he said, close to hysteria. 'How can a man continue to walk with his guts shot through and half his face missing?'

Jerry Powell frowned. The Staff Sergeant had experienced his fair share of weirdness since his deployment to Vietnam, but this was off the charts.

'Is it because we left him behind? His body, I mean. Do you think his ghost is taking revenge on us?'

'If he were after vengeance, kid, he would've gone after Charlie. They killed him, not us.'

The Staff Sergeant wasn't sure what Hudson had seen, but there was a logical explanation; there had to be. The jungle could play tricks on tired minds. In truth, the kid was fortunate not to be charged for disobeying orders. Hudson's heart was in the right place. It wasn't his fault his commanding officer was a waste of space. Leaving men behind in the field stuck in the throat.

The light was fading, and as the shadows deepened, the jungle grew more menacing by the second. Staff Sergeant Powell clapped Private Hudson on the back. 'Sit tight and keep 'em peeled, kid. Private Grant will relieve you at zero hundred hours. We'll move out at first light.' Crouching low, the sergeant disappeared into the gloom.

Randy Hudson couldn't stop thinking about what had happened. The awful image of Jo Marshal's disfigured face haunted his every waking moment. It wasn't so much the soldier's terrible injuries that disturbed Hudson. He'd seen death and destruction in all its forms since fighting the North Vietnamese. It was the man's red eyes. *He shouldn't be breathing, not after what we pumped into him.* Not for the first time since getting collared by Staff Sergeant Powell for sentry duty, Hudson gripped his crucifix.

Hudson and Grant had lost Private Marshal on their way back to camp easily enough. The afflicted GI was mutilated by a score of injuries and could only sustain an awkward lopsided amble that a three-legged water buffalo could outpace. Nonetheless, Marshal seemed determined, desperate even, to catch them no matter his speed or limitations. *Jo's setting the bar high for the walking wounded*, Hudson mused with a hysterical snigger. He didn't know whether to laugh or cry. *Hell, I'm losing my mind.* If his friend hadn't witnessed the episode, then that was precisely what Hudson would've believed. Grunts lost their minds in Vietnam every day, so why not him? But Grant's presence had put that theory to bed. *Unless Larry's crazy too?* Shaking his head, Hudson concentrated on his duty: watching the bush for the NVA… and for Marshal. *Whatever he has become.*

Night fell. Behind Hudson's position, the platoon rested back-to-back, dug into a natural hollow with weapons at hand. Ahead, the jungle was quiet. In fact, now Hudson thought about it, too quiet. Even after dark, the Vietnamese wilderness crawled with life, but the private couldn't hear so much as a cricket. Where were the croaks and whistles of the geckos and blue-eared barbets? What about the cries of big cats or the constant hum of insects? The silence was unnerving.

Marshal's bullet-mauled features flashed between Hudson's eyes. The young soldier jerked his rifle up, finger poised on the trigger. There was nothing there. *It's only your imagination, you fool.* Rubbing his tired eyes, he stared out into the shadows.

Hudson found himself thinking of home. It's what desperate soldiers do in the dead of night when they have nothing but their own thoughts for company. He missed his mom the most. She loved to fuss over him. Not like his dad; he was as tight as B Company's drill sergeant. Randy's mom sobbed her heart out for three days straight after learning that her son was being posted to Vietnam. He sighed. *God, I miss her.* Then he grinned. *But I miss her cooking more.* Cinnamon waffles, honeyed cornbread, and the best apple pie north of Fort Lauderdale.

Hudson felt something grab his shoulder. Stifling a cry, he flung himself sideways, pointing his M16 into the air.

'Jesus, Randy,' Private Grant hissed. 'It's only me.'

Hudson lowered his weapon. 'Sorry, Larry. I'm just jumpy, I guess.'

'Yeah, I know how you feel,' Grant said, settling beside his friend amongst the foliage. 'The guys think we're nuts. I'm beginning to believe they're right.' He peered over the top of the rise and out into the absolute blackness of the night. Here, where the jungle was thickest, not even starlight penetrated the treetop canopy.

'Has Dick said anything?' Hudson asked anxiously. Although the lieutenant's thoughts on their unauthorised escapade were the least of his worries.

'Nope. Dick pretends not to hear the talk. If he doesn't know about it, he doesn't have to act on it.' Lieutenant Perry didn't like confrontation, which wasn't the best of characteristics when he was a serving officer in the army, especially an army at war. 'Mind you, I did have a no-nonsense chat with Sergeant Powell.'

'Yeah, me too.'

The two young men sat silently, each staring into the darkness, searching for a blur of movement or a suspicious sound.

'Best you get your head down, Randy,' Private Grant whispered after a while. 'I'll be alright. Only a couple of hours to endure. Campbell's up next at zero two hundred.'

'Okay, Larry,' Hudson said, pushing himself to his feet. 'I doubt I'll be able to sleep, mind.' In truth, there weren't many who could find sleep in the jungle. If it weren't crazed comrades haunting their thoughts, it was fear of the enemy slitting their throats while they slept or close encounters with the local wildlife.

Grant laid a staying hand on his friend's arm. 'Wait,' he muttered. 'What's that out there? See, dead ahead?'

Private Hudson gazed into the jungle's dark depths. 'I don't see—' And then he spotted a pair of glowing red orbs hovering in the night. Hudson's breath caught in his throat. *Marshal.* He wanted to run, to bury himself in the dirt, but somehow, he knew wherever he hid, Private Marshal would find him.

Grant hauled Hudson down. 'Let's hope he hasn't clocked us.' Cautiously, the soldiers raised their heads above the slope to check. The red orbs had floated closer.

'What do we do?' Hudson hissed, aiming his rifle at the things.

Grant took a deep breath. 'We wake the platoon.' By rousing the men, at least they would find out if they were hallucinating or not. And if they weren't, Marshal would be toast, dead or alive. 'Look!' Like scarlet stars in the night sky, dozens more red orbs materialised from the darkness between the trees.

'Contact!' Private Grant bellowed, and with trembling hands and a racing pulse, he blasted his M16 into the jungle.

At once, the camp erupted into life. Staff Sergeant Powell was first on the scene. Powell sank to his knees beside the two privates, pulling a sidearm from his holster. 'What's the situation?'

Grant stopped shooting and shifted sideways to face the staff sergeant. 'Ten to twenty hostiles advancing on our position with nightscopes, sir.' He couldn't think of anything else to say.

'Nightscopes?' Staff Sergeant Powell risked poking his head above the slope. 'I don't know what they are, but they're not nightscopes, Private.'

Securing the perimeter, the platoon reported the strange phenomenon around the camp. Private Campbell reinforced Hudson, Grant, and Powell. 'Have you ever seen anything like it, Private Campbell?' Staff Sergeant Powell questioned.

Campbell shook his head in bewilderment. 'No, sir.'

It was a bizarre sight, no question. And one that left Hudson and Grant confused. Perhaps it wasn't Marshal out there? Maybe it was only a freak of nature? Fireflies, lightning bugs, or something else inhabiting the jungle they hadn't seen before?

The orbs froze, and for a time, they simply hung in the air like glowing embers suspended by the wind. Levitating higher than the others, a pair of the peculiar anomalies began gliding nearer… Suddenly, there was a thunderous roar, and the night was lit up by the flashing muzzle flame of an M60 machine gun.

'Take cover!' Staff Sergeant Powell yelled.

Bullets tore through the jungle, shredding everything in their path. Private Campbell was down. M60 rounds had nigh-on ripped the soldier's leg off at the knee.

Scrambling through the dirt, Grant was straight at the stricken GI's side, administering a hit of morphine to ease the man's wailing torment. Seconds later and the M60 stopped howling.

'Light up the sky!' Staff Sergeant Powell hollered. *Where the hell is Lieutenant Perry?*

A barrage of rocket-propelled flares launched high into the jungle's canopy. Suspended by parachutes, the flares illuminated the surrounding bush with a fluorescent glare.

'Are those our troops standing alongside Charlie?' Private Hudson questioned with bemusement.

For once, Staff Sergeant Powell was lost for words.

Then Hudson spotted Marshal, and what's more, cradling the still-smoking M60 machine gun in his massive muscular arms, he saw Curtis 'Big Bird' Goose, and at his side was a one-armed 'Jacko' Jackson.

'Corporal Lamar!' Staff Sergeant Powell yelled, rediscovering his voice.

'Sir?' came the corporal's response from somewhere in the darkness.

'Are you packing your thump-gun, kid?'

'Affirmative, sir.'

'Then hit that son of a bitch carrying our M60.'

'Sir!'

Promptly, a *thumping* noise was proceeded by a whooshing roar that fizzed through the jungle. As Hudson and Grant watched, Big Bird and Jacko were engulfed in a raging ball of fire.

'You've got to love Lamar's M79,' Private Grant muttered in awe.

'Amen to that,' Private Hudson replied, staring in absolute horror as his brothers-in-arms roasted in flame. 'Poor Goose and Jackson.'

'Whoever or whatever they are, they aren't our men, Private,' Staff Sergeant Powell stated grimly. 'Not anymore, at any rate.' Big Bird and Jacko were still standing despite getting blown up by a grenade launcher.

The red-eyed soldiers, unified in death or whatever unholy state they now found themselves bound to, lurched forward, dragging one foot in front of the other as if their ankles were shackled with ball and chain. They clambered between the trees and through the thick undergrowth heading for the platoon's position. The smouldering Big Bird led them, his body full of holes and his melted M60 welded to his blackened hands. Following Big Bird ambled at least a dozen GIs, including Marshal and a host of North Vietnamese troops—a march of empty, expressionless husks.

'Shoot them down!' Staff Sergeant Powell ordered. In the absence of the lieutenant, Powell assumed command. 'Where is Perry? Damn him!' he cried, blasting an NVA goon between his red eyes.

Death Valley echoed with a cacophony of gunfire. 2nd Platoon hurled everything they had at this depraved new enemy. Riddled with countless bullet wounds, the undying staggered onwards, a ponderous yet remorseless progression. Moaning like cattle, they appeared more like mind-dead animals than men. Some came without legs, hauling their ruined bodies through the dirt using their hands and arms or whatever hadn't been blown off like terrible writhing snakes.

A cold dread swept through Hudson's veins, chilling his heart. The urge to run was overpowering. *But there's nowhere to go.* The enemy surrounded them, and there was no escape. 'What do they want?' he whispered.

'Us, it seems, Private,' Staff Sergeant Powell replied ominously.

The hailstorm of lead slowed the horrors. But like the inevitability of death, the red eyes were unstoppable. The flares began fading, and when the all-encompassing darkness of the night returned, the things were all but on them.

A rapid succession of thumping explosions brightened the perimeter's eastern flank with blinding orange flashes. Corporal

Lamar and his M79 grenade launcher had cleared a fiery path through the enemy.

'Quickly, before they regroup, move out!' Staff Sergeant Powell yelled. 'Follow Corporal Lamar. Head due east. Rendezvous at dawn. Now run!'

Hudson and Grant hauled the semi-conscious Private Campbell upright, and with Staff Sergeant Powell bringing up the rear, they stumbled after the retreating platoon.

From the darkness, the red-eyed zombies pounced. Mutilated faces materialised from the shadows, their cold dead hands grabbing feverishly at the living. Staff Sergeant Powell's pistol flashed and banged, but suddenly he was gone, snatched, and dragged screaming into the undergrowth.

'They've got Powell!' Hudson cried in despair.

The Big Marine

Doubled over, Private Hudson gasped for breath. 'Thank God,' he murmured. 'Somehow, I'm still alive.' Beads of sweat dripped from the tip of his nose, falling into the chill water swirling around his feet. Every muscle in his body burned with fatigue. He hadn't stopped running, not while it was still dark. Now the promise of a new dawn lifted his spirits, a rekindling of hope when there was none during the dead of night. The brightening skyline beckoned the young soldier eastward. He staggered onwards, his weary feet splashing through the shallow stream.

It had all happened so fast. After Powell had been taken, Campbell was snatched, too, pulled from Hudson's arms and dragged into the darkness just like the staff sergeant before him. During the chaos, Hudson had lost touch with the platoon. In truth, he was lucky to have escaped with his life. *There was nothing I could have done*, Hudson told himself. There was no going back, not now. Campbell was gone, and so was Powell.

As he wandered the snaking creek bed, the jungle began re-emerging from the darkness, a blur of ill-defined shapes looming from the gloom. Through the trees, the dawn intensified, lancing through the jungle's thick canopy to grace the horizon. More than once, Hudson thought he saw the enemy within the half-light, Viet Cong, NVA, or worse, the red-eyed demons who prowled the night. Yet as he passed them, they were nothing more than trees and shrubs lining the riverbank. The shapes weren't always nightmarish. Sometimes he saw faces: President Johnson, John Wayne, Bob Dylan. Once, he even saw Audrey Hepburn staring back at him; although he would have preferred Marilyn Monroe, God rest her soul.

Just keep going, he told himself, checking over his shoulder for the hundredth time. *One foot in front of the other*. His feet were numb with cold and his thoughts whirling in turmoil. Hudson trod the placid waterway for another hour or two, perhaps more, until he finally stumbled upon his platoon. Occupying a sloping bend of the creek bed, a forlorn gathering of broken men slumped upon the riverbank.

As soon as Hudson shuffled into view, an arsenal of weaponry was instantly pointed his way, including his best friend's M16. 'It's alright,' he heard Grant say. 'It's only Randy.'

Nonetheless, the platoon kept their guns trained on the private. 'Check his eyes,' Corporal Lamar ordered, twitching his grenade launcher at the young soldier.

Hudson held his hands up. 'For God's sake, it's me,' he protested.

Grant squinted into the weak, early light. 'No devil eyes,' he confirmed, lowering his rifle.

Relaxing, 2nd Platoon returned to their sombre reflection.

'Is there anyone else?' Corporal Lamar questioned.

Wading nearer, Hudson shook his head. 'I think I'm the last.'

Corporal Lamar nodded grimly before moving away to confer with Private Hicks.

Hudson collapsed onto the riverbank beside Grant. 'Any sign of Lieutenant Perry?' he asked.

'Nothing,' Grant said. 'Nor Griffin.'

The loss of Campbell weighed heavily on Hudson's shoulders. *If only I'd been faster, Campbell might still be alive.* Although missing the best part of a leg was always going to prove problematic for Campbell, not that the undying seemed to move very fast.

While wallowing in self-pity, Hudson's eyes wandered. He noted how the platoon's survivors exhibited the same haunted expression etched into their bloodied, dirt-smeared faces. It was a combination of loss, fear, and disbelieving horror. Their wide eyes stared unblinking into nothingness, but Hudson knew their minds were reeling in shock, playing out what they had witnessed over and over. *If war isn't bad enough*, Hudson mused dejectedly. He couldn't find the words. This was war beyond comprehension, beyond the realms of logic. *The dead walking. It's the stuff of nightmares and horror stories.*

'Come on, off your buts,' Corporal Lamar said, hustling the troops into action. 'We need to keep moving.' None of them required reminding of what stalked them.

Leaving the stream behind, the platoon returned beneath the trees. In daylight, the creek bed was dangerously exposed and was leading them too far off course. To reach the extraction site, Corporal Lamar guessed they needed to march at least ten klicks east before cutting north for another two. Without Sergeant Griffin and his radio, there was zero chance of calling in an emergency air-lift courtesy of the 7th Cavalry's fleet of 'Huey' helicopters or air support if things turned really crazy. *Not that blowing up the enemy will do any good when they're already dead*, Hudson thought darkly, trudging behind his comrades. *Still, I'd like to see them walk after being napalmed.*

The remainder of the morning was spent hacking a route through dense vegetation, but shortly after noon, Corporal Lamar raised a clenched fist, halting the platoon in their tracks.

Here the trees thinned, giving way to an exposed area of grass and shrubland. The corporal eyed the landscape ahead with suspicion before signalling the men to keep low and advance with caution. Reaching higher ground, Corporal Lamar stopped again. From the summit of a gentle ridge, he pointed his grenade launcher toward the bottom of the slope.

Peering through the shimmering heat, Hudson rolled his eyes in disbelief. Hunkered together within a small grove of stunted saplings and coffee bushes were Lieutenant Perry and Sergeant Griffin. 'They haven't even noticed us,' Hudson whispered to Grant, belly down in the dirt beside him.

Corporal Lamar was about to order the men forward when he noticed movement within the treeline beyond Lieutenant Perry and Sergeant Griffin's position. 'Charlie'.

Events are going to get really interesting really quickly, Hudson thought, watching the camouflaged helmets of North Vietnamese soldiers bobbing between the trees.

Perry and Griffin were preoccupied with the radio. Hudson could hear the device crackling and hissing from where he lay hidden. Hudson shook his head. *If they don't move, they're dead.* The officers appeared ignorant of the proximity of both 2nd Platoon and the suspected NVA patrol fast approaching from the opposite direction.

Suddenly, Corporal Lamar surged to his feet. 'Lieutenant Perry!' he hollered. 'Get the hell out of there!' All thoughts of concealing their whereabouts went up in smoke.

To a man, 2nd Platoon clambered up, waving their guns and helmets above their heads to attract the attention of the two stranded soldiers. But by the time the officers noticed, the NVA were streaming from the jungle with their whistles and Ak-47s blaring.

Dropping to the ground, 2nd Platoon prepared for battle, leaving Lieutenant Perry and Sergeant Griffin dithering in no man's land. They couldn't decide whether to make a desperate last-minute dash for the platoon's lines or remain where they were crouched behind the bushes.

'God damn!' Lieutenant Perry cursed. 'It's too late.' Accepting the situation, the two men raised their rifles and faced the enemy.

The rattle of gunfire erupted like a breaking thunderstorm engulfing the stranded US soldiers within a hail of lead. Rounds hammered their position, showering them in shredded bark and Vietnamese dirt. Perry and Griffin could do little else except bury their faces in the grass and pray they didn't take a bullet.

Hudson targeted a North Vietnamese soldier charging through the grass with a glinting bayonet protruding from his AK-47. Aiming at the man's chest, Hudson felt for the trigger of his M16. 'Just a little closer,' he murmured, tracking the enemy soldier as he hurtled toward Perry and Griffin. 'Got you.' He squeezed the trigger, but a flash of light blinded him. When he could see again, a strange man was standing in the way of his shot, slap bang in the middle of no man's land beside the stranded officers. *Who the hell is that?*

The man was a big marine and how he wasn't dead was a mystery. As bold as brass and without regard for the gunfire pouring past him, he towered over Lieutenant Perry and Sergeant Griffin. *How are the bullets not hitting him?* Hudson mused, dumbfounded.

Spontaneously, both sides ceased firing. It was bizarre. The NVA soldiers, screaming for blood seconds earlier, now lowered their machine guns and gazed at this newcomer with bemusement. It was almost as if the big marine had cast a spell on them. Compelled from their position, 2nd Platoon emerged from cover and hesitantly began advancing into the long grass.

Hudson couldn't explain what was happening. Two opposing enemies hellbent on one another's destruction now meandered toward the other, with all thoughts of killing forgotten. *What's going on?* Although Hudson questioned the platoon's actions, he couldn't stop himself from joining the others gathering around the newcomer. On one side of the big marine crowded 2nd Platoon, and on the other, the NVA patrol.

Lieutenant Perry rose to his feet before saluting. 'What's this all about, sir?' he asked, eyeing the enemy troops with distrust.

The big marine, who Hudson saw was a captain, didn't answer. Instead, he beckoned an enemy soldier to his side. The man was short and slender with dark eyes and hair. *To be honest, just like all the others*, Hudson thought.

'This is Dinh Son Kim of the North Vietnamese Army's 9th Battalion. He is the commanding officer of this patrol.'

Dinh Son Kim bowed.

Richard Perry nodded brusquely.

'How do you know these men, Captain?' Sergeant Griffin questioned, narrowing his beady eyes, his fingers caressing the trigger of his M16.

'I don't,' the big marine replied. 'They are merely obeying the orders of a superior officer.'

'But who is their superior officer?' Hudson asked.

The soldier fixed his blue eyes on the young private. They shone like sapphires, true and bright. It was as if the man's gaze laid bare Randy's innermost thoughts, which Randy didn't much like. 'I am,' the big marine declared.

If the soldiers of 2nd Platoon had been confused before, they were now lost entirely.

'But you're one of us,' Hudson muttered feebly.

'I am Dinh Son Kim's superior officer just as I am Lieutenant Perry's,' the big marine continued as if he were explaining rudimentary math to a kindergarten class. 'I know the situation is strange for you, but be assured, I am here for your own good. Evil stalks this valley.'

The big marine paused to gauge the soldiers' response. Mentioning evil usually gave humans 'the fear', which, perversely, he rather enjoyed observing. Sweeping his sapphire stare over them, he decided to increase the jeopardy. 'You know what I speak of; I can see it in your eyes. There is something deep in the jungle, and it cares not which side you fight on or for your war. It cares only for itself and the destruction of everything in its path. This evil must be stopped, but to achieve victory, we must cooperate. Although I cannot guarantee your survival.' *That should get them going*, the big marine mused wryly.

On both sides, the men erupted with outrage. Honouring a ceasefire was one thing, but fighting together was unthinkable. It amused the big marine that the proclaimed *evil* wasn't questioned, only the inconvenience of a potential partnership. *Humans never change*, he thought. *They are quite content murdering each other even when presented with a common enemy*. Yet, for their many faults, he couldn't help feeling for them. They weren't all to blame. The Devil's influence was a constant battle for them to endure.

'Fighting back-to-back takes trust,' Corporal Lamar explained bitterly, eyeing the North Vietnamese as if they had just slid from the rear end of a giant rat. 'And the day I trust Charlie is the day hell freezes over.'

'This *is* that day, Denzel Lamar,' the big marine declared ominously, his blue eyes glowering at the corporal. 'Yet Hell won't freeze over. It will creep up on you in the dead of night and drag you screaming into the abyss.'

The captain's chilling remarks silenced the men. 'Now you face a new foe. If ignored, everything you hold dear will fall to its malevolence. I cannot complete this task alone. I require your help.'

Actually, I probably can do it alone, the big marine mused. In fairness, there wasn't much he couldn't handle. Nonetheless, here was an opportunity to heal a few rifts and have some fun along the way. And in any case, he doubted the assignment would be anything exciting; more's the pity. *Most likely, it will involve incinerating a few zombies and a Hellgate to close. Nothing too taxing.*

Hudson stared at the North Vietnamese. Like 2nd Platoon, they were young men who seemed every bit as scarred by the big marine's revelation as he and his comrades. Hudson gripped his crucifix. He'd seen enough to know the truth of the captain's words. What they faced was beyond the wars of men. This was a war of a higher purpose, good versus evil in its purest form. This was biblical. 'I'm in,' the private declared.

The big marine grinned. 'Splendid!'

The Pit

Even though they didn't understand, the soldiers followed Private Hudson's example and pledged themselves to the big marine's cause. As yet, they were unsure in what form their support or the marine's cause would take, but each and every one of them recognised the Devil's work when they saw it.

'We must locate the source of this evil and tear it out by the root,' the big marine announced, his blue eyes gleaming.

'Search and destroy, grunts. Search and destroy!' Corporal Lamar was eager for some action, and by the troops' response, so were they.

Private Hicks rattled his gun like a sabre. 'Amen to that, Corporal!'

'I will not risk your lives needlessly,' the captain continued. 'Nonetheless, I will require two volunteers to assist me in scouting the enemy's position and strength.' He eyed the troops for signs of willing participants, but despite the metaphoric *sabre rattling*, he wasn't feeling the love. 'In the circumstances, I think it best the volunteers are chosen from opposing sides.' He didn't want to be accused of favouritism.

Hudson raised a hand. 'I'll go, sir,' he said. 'Although I'm not sure what use I'll be.' He hoped the deed would lessen the guilt he felt for what happened to Campbell.

'Are you mad, Randy?' Private Grant blurted. 'You've seen what's out there. We should run while we've got the chance.'

Grant was less than convinced by the situation and the big marine's fanciful story.

The captain's left eye began twitching. He had an innate dislike for cowards and defeatists, and it required all his resolve not to resort to extreme violence. 'Tell me, Private, who will stand in our stead if we run?'

'I don't care so long as it's not me,' Grant muttered, staring at the ground.

'You should care,' the big marine stated. *Because if you don't, I'll roast you alive, you damnable wretch!* Threatening the private, even if the outburst was only imagined inside his head, made him feel considerably better.

While talking himself out of burning the young man to ash—an act that would have undoubtedly condemned his immortal soul to eternal damnation, or at least until he'd atoned for his sins, which, if his current sentence was comparable, would be another few thousand years or so—a North Vietnamese soldier stepped from the ranks to approach the captain. 'I accept, Commander,' he announced, accompanying his words with a sharp salute.

For now, thanks to the NVA recruit, Private Grant was spared the big marine's retribution. 'Ensign Dang Van Fu, you make your regiment proud,' the captain declared, dipping his head in respect. Then he spread his arms wide and addressed the two opposing forces. 'Await our return. Be watchful. If the undead come again, fall back. We'll find you.'

Wasting no time, the soldiers got to work digging a defensive perimeter into the earth. One half was assigned to the US Infantry, and the other, to their new allies, the NVA.

Before the big marine and his two volunteers departed on their mission, the captain took Lieutenant Perry aside. 'I know what you did,' he accused the officer once the two were alone.

'I don't understand, sir?' the lieutenant answered. His face was a picture of innocence. 'I haven't done anything.'

The big marine felt another bout of left-eye-twitch coming on and decided liars should join cowards and defeatists on his growing list of villainous traits. And as far as he could tell, the lieutenant was all three. 'When the dead came, you and your sergeant fled, abandoning your men to their fate.'

Lieutenant Perry suddenly looked very ill. 'In order to operate the radio and call for help, we thought it prudent to find higher ground.'

Utterly pathetic, the big marine concluded. How many lives had been lost to poor leadership during Earth's countless wars? It didn't bear thinking about. 'So you believed depriving your platoon of its commanding officer while engaged in battle was a wise course of action?'

The lieutenant didn't have the words to answer, nor did he have the courage to meet the captain's sapphire gaze.

The big marine sighed. Despite his fondness for old-school morals and a no-nonsense criminal system that really ought to include immediate incineration without reprieve, he was feeling unexpectedly forgiving. And besides, Lieutenant Perry wasn't as hopeless as he or his men seemed to think.

'I am not here to judge you, Richard,' the captain spoke softly. 'I know you battle your demons daily. You fight your fears and anxieties, and they often beat you into submission. Do not let them. Make a stand with me here in the jungle. Show your soldiers what sort of man you truly are. Find your heart. I know you can.'

The meeting left the lieutenant feeling strangely affected by the big marine's words. He couldn't explain why, but it was as if the man had unburdened him in some way. The tightness that had gripped his soul for so long had eased. *How did he know those things?* The captain was right. It was time to face his fears, but the truth of it was he didn't know how.

The big marine and his unlikely recruits ventured into the jungle. Unlikely because, before today, such a partnership was inconceivable. Yet now, because of a perverse twist of fate, the two adversaries were united for the common good. A powerful and sinister new enemy had emerged, and only together was there a chance of survival. Even so, trust was not easily gained, and the two soldiers spent as much time watching each other as they did their increasingly precarious surroundings.

The sun had risen. The heat began building beneath the leafy canopy above. Strangely, there were no buzzing flies or chirping birds in the treetops. In fact, there was no sign of life at all. Gripping their weapons with trembling hands, the two young soldiers stared into the jungle's shadowed depths with wide, fearful eyes.

Suddenly, Ensign Fu became animated, and without warning, his hand snaked out, grabbing the big marine's muscular arm and hauling him to a stop. 'Ngừng lại!' the North Vietnamese soldier yelled in his native tongue.

Private Hudson turned his M16 on the NVA trooper. 'What's he saying?' he demanded, his finger twitching on the trigger.

The big marine pushed Hudson's rifle down. 'Have faith,' he whispered.

Ensign Fu hastened past the pair. 'Bẫy,' he announced, frantically jabbing his AK-47 at the leaf-strewn ground in front of his feet. 'Cạm bẫy!'

'A booby trap,' the captain translated. 'A spear pit covered with branches.'

Private Hudson stared at Ensign Fu accusingly. The thought of being impaled by spears at the bottom of a hole was as disconcerting as facing the undead... nearly. Traps were the lowest form of warfare. Nonetheless, Randy dipped his head in silent thanks.

'Trust must be earned,' the big marine said, carefully circumnavigating the deadly pit before briskly setting off again.

'Who are you?' Hudson asked, hurrying to catch up. The captain looked and talked like a US Marine, but something about him wasn't quite right. Firstly, he didn't carry a weapon, not one that Randy could see, at any rate. *What sort of soldier doesn't take a weapon to war?* And how the man hadn't gotten shot earlier when, for all the world, it seemed impossible not to was baffling. *He should be dead, but there's not a scratch on him.*

'I am a soldier like you, Randy,' the big marine answered.

Hudson narrowed his eyes. 'I'm not sure you are. At least, not any soldier I've met before. What's your name?' For some bizarre reason, he couldn't recall anyone asking before now, and the man hadn't offered.

The big marine turned, his blue eyes shining. 'My name is Cassius.'

Private Hudson frowned. 'Captain Cassius?'

Cassius smiled. 'Yes, that will do.'

Hudson peered at Dang Van Fu and then back at Captain Cassius. 'How come he obeys you like one of his own?'

'Because, Randy, he sees me as one of his own.' *This boy has almost got a brain*, Cassius mused, pleasantry surprised. In his experience, grunts were not known for their mental aptitude.

'I don't understand. What are you saying?'

'To you, I'm a captain in the Marines, and to Dang, I'm a commander in the NVA.' *Let's see how his brain deals with that little bombshell.* Cassius was, of course, playing games, but entertainment was so hard to come by in his line of work.

'How can we both see you as someone different?' Private Hudson pressed, desperate for answers. 'Who are you, *really?*'

'In truth, Randy, I *am* a soldier like you and Dang. I am a specialist, you might say. A hunter of things that do not belong here. And yes, I am not who I seem. Yet do not fret. I'm one of the good guys, I promise.' *There, the cat's out of the bag.* Well, perhaps its furry little head and two front paws. Enough, at any rate, to nudge the soldier in the right direction. Cassius could almost see the cogs turning inside the boy's head. Admittedly, knowing the truth wasn't always for the best. Cassius had lost count of the times humans fainted after learning he'd been sent by Heaven. In fact, on occasion, they would drop stone dead at his feet. *Not that I have seen Heaven for nearly two thousand years*, he mused dolefully.

Private Hudson fell in line behind Ensign Fu and Captain Cassius—or whoever he was? His thoughts were spinning. Explanations swirled inside his mind, but each was as unlikely as the last. Who was this imposter? By his own omission, he was neither a US Marine nor an NVA commander. Nonetheless, despite the man's secrets and peculiarities,

Hudson trusted him. In truth, it was more than trust. It was a fierce devotion he couldn't explain or justify.

Suddenly, Cassius hauled his recruits into the foliage, concealing them within the leafy embrace of a bamboo thicket.

'What are we hiding from?' Hudson whispered breathlessly.

Putting a finger to his lips, Cassius nodded into the trees ahead.

At once, the hairs on the back of the private's neck stood on end. Not twenty paces away, a pair of NVA soldiers materialised from the jungle. They walked with a ponderous, awkward gait, looking like they'd indulged in way too much bourbon after an all-night disco and a no-nonsense bar brawl, and even at twenty paces, Hudson could see their eyes glowing red. *The undead!*

Fu gasped. He recognised these men, but whoever they once were, now they were dead men walking.

'What are they hauling?' Hudson whispered. He saw flashes of orange through the bushes and then… *Was that a growl?*

Fu had a better view. If seeing his zombified comrades wasn't disturbing enough, then the sight of what they transported behind them increased the feeling ten-fold. 'A tiger,' Fu muttered in astonishment.

Grasping the animal by its hind legs, the undead dragged it through the jungle on its back. The tiger was injured, but not so badly to prevent it from lashing out at its captors. Its huge paws inflicted deep, raking wounds into their flesh. But lacerations to a dead man are water off a duck's back.

The tiger and its abductors disappeared into the trees. Immediately after, a procession of undead American and North Vietnamese soldiers followed, each carrying or dragging some form of jungle creature: snakes, bears, and even a water buffalo.

'Let us see where this ungodly troop leads us,' Cassius whispered.

As quiet as mice, the three soldiers crept unnoticed through the undergrowth in the undead's wake. In reality, such was the uproar caused by the stomping march of this lifeless army and their disgruntled cargo that a stampeding herd of elephants might easily have trailed them without detection.

After another hour spent skulking on hands and knees amongst the jungle's depths, Cassius paused their pursuit. Beyond them, the terrain opened out again, and at the centre of a cleared expanse, there was a giant gaping hole into which the undead tossed their offerings.

'What are they doing?' Hudson watched as a terribly mauled zombie soldier wrestled a lively leopard into position above the pit. Grappling with one another, both man and beast disappeared inside.

Cassius sighed lamentably. He hadn't bargained for this. 'They feed what is growing within.'

Hudson and Fu traded a horrified glance.

'Something is living inside that hole?' Hudson whispered anxiously. What manner of thing could stomach tigers and leopards… and water buffalo? He couldn't begin to imagine. Whatever lurked inside the pit wasn't natural.

'I'm afraid so. We have found the source of the evil plaguing the jungle. It is what I hoped not to find.' For the first time in an age, Cassius was troubled. 'We must return to the others at once. This foe is beyond us.'

'Quái vật,' Ensign Fu muttered, his voice quivering with fear.

Cassius nodded grimly. 'Yes, Dang. Quái vật.'

'What does that mean?'

'Monster.'

All at once, the undead congregating at the pit's edge jerked their lifeless heads toward the bamboo grove where Cassius and his two allies sheltered.

'They sense our presence,' Cassius warned. 'We should leave and swiftly.'

The undead hauling wildlife dropped their squirming loads and reached for their guns instead. A barrage of bullets tore into the undergrowth, but the spies had fled. On rotting legs, the zombies of Death Valley lurched into the jungle to begin the pursuit.

Arc Light

Something was coming, not just yet but very soon… something big.

The twentieth century had seen war after war, and this conflict in Vietnam was the latest addition to a disheartening trend. Demonic activity was on the rise. Cassius hadn't witnessed anything so intense since the Dark Ages when the Devil held sway. *The new millennium fast approaches*, he mused. *And the Fallen One prepares his forces.*

As each century dies, the Dream War begins, good versus evil, with the victor granted power for a hundred years. Yet once every thousand, the Dream War assumes special significance, a chance for the Devil to free himself from Hell.

In times of peril, there is much to gain. And here, in the sprawling jungles of Vietnam, Cassius was presented with the chance to shine. He could almost smell redemption in the warm, humid air.

The red sun was falling into the west when Cassius and his recruits returned to camp. He half expected to find piles of bullet-ridden corpses lying face down amidst the swaying grass. Yet low and behold, not only had the reluctant allies refrained from slaughtering each other, but their fortifications were complete. *After all this time, humans never cease to amaze me*, Cassius mused. *Flawed by their inability to accept their differences yet capable of moments of greatness.*

The big marine summoned Lieutenant Richard Perry and Lieutenant Dinh Son Kim to gather their troops. 'We don't have much time,' Cassius announced gravely. 'We have a lead on them, but the dead are on their way.' The temptation to sugar-coat the news was compelling, but he decided to let them know what they were up against. *Prepare for the worst, hope for the best… or something like that.*

Unease rippled through the ranks. Twenty-four hours of hell had shredded the men's nerves, and now they had just been told that they would face the dreaded zombies again.

'What did you find, Captain?' Lieutenant Perry asked. 'What's out there?' Although the lieutenant sounded confident, his eyes betrayed his true feelings—a growing panic was rising behind them, threatening to overwhelm and overthrow him in a heartbeat.

'At the heart of the jungle, we discovered a nesting site. Into a vast pit, the undead cast their prey, nurturing the demon inside with flesh and bone. The undead are its workers, sent forth to harvest the life from the land. Having consumed its fill, the creature will transform into something terrible. If the worst happens, one thing is clear, Lieutenant. We will need bigger guns.'

Cassius was met with dreaded silence. He grimaced. *Too much detail? Perhaps a sprinkling of sugar might have been warranted after all. Well, at least they won't be under any illusions.*

And nor would they be. Following the captain's harrowing update, the men appeared resigned to a grim fate. Nonetheless, as quickly as their doom was accepted, the men found their resolve. If they were going to die, they were damn well going to die fighting.

'How do we kill this thing?' Lieutenant Kim hissed, eager to take the demon down with him.

'Yes, Lieutenant Kim, that's the spirit!' Cassius praised, and then his sapphire eyes narrowed. 'I have just the thing… Napalm.'

'Hell yeah! Let's roast the ugly whoreson before it crawls from its damn hole!' Corporal Lamar's enthusiasm was met by an eruption of hoots and whoops from the US soldiers. The NVA troops were less keen.

Understandable, Cassius thought. They'd witnessed the terrible destructive power of the incendiary bombs first-hand. Yet the effectiveness of the weapon couldn't be denied, nor its potential to end this nightmare before it became an awful reality.

'Napalm is abhorrent,' the captain declared. 'Nonetheless, in the circumstances, a necessary evil. The demon's insatiable appetite has scoured the surrounding habitat of life. As such, the decision to deploy the weapon is made easier, but I can assure you that it is not done lightly.'

Lieutenant Perry cleared his throat noisily.

'Yes, Lieutenant?'

'I hate to rain on your parade, but to call an airstrike, we need a working radio, and ours doesn't.'

'Ah, yes. Am I correct in thinking the device requires altitude to function?'

Sergeant Griffin, 2nd Platoon's radio operator, pushed himself through the throng of soldiers until he stood before the captain. 'Gaining a little height should do the trick,' he confirmed. 'Normally, the radio works well enough at ground level, but I suspect your friend in its hole is interfering with the signal.'

'How much height might suffice, do you think, Sergeant?'

Sergeant Griffin thought for a moment. 'A few hundred feet or so will do.'

Cassius smirked, grabbed the sergeant by the arms, and launched them into the sky.

Griffin was too shocked to scream. The air rushed past him like a hurricane. His eyes bulged, his heart skipped at least seven beats, and the skin on his face felt as though it were being peeled from his skull with a paint stripper. Abruptly, they jerked to a stop.

'Three hundred feet, or thereabouts,' Cassius stated casually. 'Shall I hand you your radio?'

The big marine acted as if hovering above the jungle like some damn comic book superhero with nothing but thin air between them and a disagreeable union with the ground was an everyday occurrence. 'For god's sake, man!' Griffin blurted hysterically. 'How are you making this happen?'

'I understand your concerns, Sergeant, but ignore the hows, whys, and what-ifs and concentrate on the task at hand.' Mortals could be so dramatic sometimes. Keeping a calm head in moments of chaos was a skill few of them ever learned. *Instead, they break into a song and dance whenever things don't go according to plan.*

The sergeant's wide, horrified eyes stared down at the trees three hundred feet below his feet.

'Look at me, Ray,' Cassius demanded. There was no time for theatrics.

The captain's tone distracted Sergeant Griffin, and his head snapped around, eyes front and centre.

'Good, man. Now, don't be alarmed, but I'm going to let you go. I promise you won't fall.'

Sergeant Griffin began whimpering.

'Ready?'

The sergeant shook his head with such intensity Cassius feared the man's neck might snap. 'Are you insane? Of course, I'm not ready!'

Ignoring Sergeant Griffin's protests, Cassius withdrew his hands, leaving the bemused soldier hanging in mid-air.

'How?'

'Time is running out, Ray.'

The enemy was here, an army of the dead sent to snuff out the last remnants of life in Death Valley. Cassius couldn't see them through the jungle's impenetrable canopy, not yet, but he could feel their unholy presence spreading amongst the trees like a poisonous cloud.

Cassius pulled the radio from the sergeant's backpack and thrust it into the soldier's hands. He pointed to a noticeable depression on the horizon where the jungle's trees were flattened. 'Call the airstrike, Ray.'

'M-m-m-map,' Sergeant Griffin stuttered. He'd noticed movement at the edge of the clearing, twisted shadows creeping through the trees where the vegetation thinned. The presence of the dead focussed his mind, and with the radio floating beside him, he snatched the map from the captain's hands before pinpointing the target. 'This is 1ST Battalion, 7TH Cavalry, B Company requesting an urgent ARC LIGHT run!'

Suddenly a hole appeared in the unfurled map, and then another, and as the sergeant relayed the coordinates, more shots whistled through the air. 'Come on, come on, come on,' Sergeant Griffin muttered anxiously, waiting for a response from HQ. 'Answer, God damn you!'

A bullet hit Cassius, ricocheting off his forehead before zipping perilously close to the sergeant's left ear. Cassius shrugged. 'Thick skin,' he explained.

At last, the radio crackled into life once more. Confirmation was received, and the airstrike was authorised with immediate effect.

'Done,' Sergeant Griffin declared, bracing himself for the descent. The captain regripped his arms, and soon after, the sergeant experienced a horrible lurching sensation. After what only felt like a heartbeat, they were safely on their feet in the camp once more. Sergeant Griffin exhaled a relieved sigh. 'Thank the Lord,' he praised, sinking to his knees and kissing the soil beneath his boots.

'Yes, thank him… but thank me more, hey?' Cassius said with a wink.

Slack-jawed and numbed to the core, the soldiers stared at the captain as if he were the Messiah himself.

'Yes, yes, I know. Well, I'm an angel, so get used to it. And luckily for you, I'm the "annihilate thy enemies into dust" and not the "let's hold hands and warble a hymn until they all go away" variety. The last thing you need right now is a bible-bashing, sandal-wearing cheek kisser. I'm Old Testament, an eye for an eye, a tooth for a tooth… and damnation to anyone he says different.'

Cassius took a breath. *Too much?* He just couldn't help himself sometimes. 'Anyway, enough about me,' he said, an awkward smile twitching at the corner of his mouth. 'It seems we have visitors… the dead are here.'

The soldiers didn't know what to make of the big marine's outburst, and if it hadn't been for his Superman impersonation, they would have thought him mentally disturbed.

But there was no time for explanations.

'2nd Platoon,' Lieutenant Perry yelled, 'hold tight and put down anything that comes out of those trees.' *That's it, Richard,* he told himself. *You can do it. Deep breaths, brave face.*

The Platoon slid into their freshly dug foxholes. Stacking their magazines close, they readied themselves for action. Lieutenant Kim ordered his troops into position, and soon their trenches bristled with bayonets sticking from AK-47 machine guns.

Cassius leapt into a foxhole beside Hudson and Grant. The soldiers glared at the man as if he were on fire. 'Haven't you seen an angel before?'

The two privates shook their heads.

Cassius grinned. 'You're in for a treat.'

Private Hudson's admiration for this so-called angel was momentarily tempered by a sudden burst of nervous animosity. 'Why didn't you fly us back from the pit?' he demanded. 'I nearly got shot… twice!'

Not for the first time, Cassius was impressed by the young man's spunk. In fairness, it was a good point that deserved an honest answer. 'My apologies, Randy, but what the monster's minions see, it sees. I dare not risk the creature accelerating its metamorphosis before having the chance to hit the thing with something big.' By the look on Hudson's face, Cassius wasn't convinced he'd understood. *Yet perhaps enough to appease his anger.*

The sun fell into the trees' leafy clutches, and the jungle began to darken. The soldiers searched the terrain, peering from their hastily constructed defences. Then they saw them; dark shapes emerging from between the gnarled boughs and swaying branches.

'Here they come,' Cassius warned. 'Aim for their eyes.' It was good advice. Glowing red, they were easy to spot in the failing light.

All at once, gunfire exploded from the foxholes and trenches, a hail of screaming bullets unleashed into the gloom. The undead lumbered straight into the eye of a storm. Peppered with lead, their breathless bodies were hammered from their feet. Some managed to stumble onwards but were soon hit with an onslaught of machine gun fire from AK-47s and M16s and a thunderous bombardment from Corporal Lamar's grenade launcher. When the dust settled, the dead were where they belonged, in the dirt.

Hudson and Grant cheered, as did their comrades hidden in the darkness. 'I shouldn't get too excited,' Cassius warned.

Private Hicks yelled in terror. 'They're getting back up!'

Cassius shrugged his shoulders apologetically. 'See, I told you.'

The zombies hauled their bullet-ridden carcases upright before lurching forward as if nothing had befallen them.

'Keep knocking them down,' Cassius yelled. 'We need to hold them off until the airstrike arrives.' It was a waiting game.

But perhaps he could buy some much-needed time. *And have a little fun in the process.*

'Where are you going?' Hudson demanded. 'You won't last five seconds out there on your own!'

The big marine winked. 'Watch and learn, Private. Watch and learn.'

As night closed in around them, so did the relentless army of the dead. However, Heaven had sent a battle angel, and the darkness was dispelled by pulsing blasts of holy light.

Private Hudson's mouth gaped open like a Mississippi bass fresh out of the river as Captain Cassius shot rays of gleaming white light from his hands into the ranks of the undying. Each searing beam found its mark, and each mark was incinerated into oblivion.

'That's why he doesn't need a weapon,' Hudson muttered in amazement. 'He is one.'

The night was filled with the constant roaring of explosions and lit by a firework display of fizzing tracer fire and angel light. However, despite the firepower dispatched into their unholy ranks, the zombies kept coming.

North Vietnamese soldiers added their screams to the chaos. The undead had breached their defences, and now Lieutenant Dinh Son Kim and his men fought hand-to-hand in the trenches.

'Come on, you two. We're needed,' Cassius said, ducking his head into Hudson and Grant's foxhole. Scrambling after the angel, the soldiers crossed the short but dangerously exposed terrain between them and the NVA defences.

'Heads down!' Cassius cried as bullets whizzed past them in the dark. Sliding into the North Vietnamese trench, they found themselves surrounded by the crimson eyes of the dead.

Hudson blasted a faceless zombie into pulp and then another, riddling its animated corpse with lead. More were coming, and the monsters he'd just put down were already twitching upright again. Icy hands grabbed him from behind, pulling him backwards. Hudson spun, skewering the cold-blooded soldier through the guts. He gasped. The flame-ravaged features of Curtis 'Big Bird' Goose stared down at him with glaring red eyes.

Big Bird smashed his half-arm-half-M60 limb at the private. Hudson flung himself aside, but Big Bird's sidekick, 'Jacko' Jackson, was on him in a heartbeat. The undead's gruesome face pressed close, blackened teeth ready to tear at his flesh. Suddenly, there was a dazzling flash, and Jackson was gone, vaporised into dust. Yet before Hudson could thank Cassius, Big Bird returned to finish him.

Ensign Fu leapt at the giant zombie, knocking him into the dirt. He clambered onto the thing and thrust his bayonet deep into its festering heart, but Big Bird wouldn't die. Fleshless fingers clamped around Fu's throat, squeezing the life from the young soldier.

'No!' Hudson screamed. He snatched up Fu's discarded machine gun and emptied the weapon's magazine into Big Bird's decaying body, but he was too late. Hudson staggered away from the twitching corpses. He'd lost sight of Cassius, and the last time he'd seen Grant, he had disappeared beneath a score of zombies. Fu was dead, but being 'dead' wasn't going to stop Big Bird. The soldier's decimated body began hauling itself erect. 'We can't win,' Hudson whispered despairingly.

The US infantry poured into the NVA trenches, desperate to save their new allies and themselves from the horrors of the night.

Lieutenant Perry and Sergeant Griffin fought back-to-back, keeping the undead's reaching hands at arm's length with controlled blasts of M16 fire. Corporal Lamar launched his last grenade, blowing a pair of zombies sky-high. Out of ammo, Lieutenant Kim drew his machete, ready to gut anything that wasn't breathing. Angel light flashed again and again, searing the lifeless soldiers from existence, but it wasn't enough. There were too many.

Then above the mayhem and carnage, those still breathing heard the unmistakable hum of eight turbojet engines. Rumbling high overhead was a United States Air Force B-52 Stratofortress, and it was music to the ears.

A roaring explosion illuminated the jungle with raging flame. The sky blazed yellow and orange. In unison, the zombies' crimson eyes faded, and the army of the dead fell.

Cassius gazed into the fire-lit night. 'It is over,' he whispered.

Apocalypse Dawn

The horizon glowed red, a false dawn summoning the soldiers north. Back at the camp, they had laid the dead to rest, US troopers side by side with the North Vietnamese. They'd found Marshal, Campbell, and Hudson's best friend Larry Grant among the host of bodies.

Now they're at peace, Hudson thought. He'd buried Larry beside Dang Van Fu, who had saved him from Big Bird during the night. Before yesterday, who would have believed an NVA soldier would have given his life to save a US grunt? If Randy had learned one thing from this ordeal, it was the simple truth that soldiers were just people, no matter their uniform. *We're all just following orders.* Once this strange mission was over and normal relations between the two warring nations resumed, he wasn't sure how he would be able to continue as before, yet he knew he must. Rightly or wrongly, wars are begun and ended by the powers that be. Regular folk can do little else but trust in their leaders.

Angel Cassius guided the battle-weary troops deep into the jungle, a sombre parade through the lifeless heart of Death Valley. Although victorious, the experience left the soldiers physically and emotionally drained. Facing the undead was harrowing, but facing your undead friends was worse.

Once the creature's death was confirmed, the brief alliance would part ways. Lieutenant Perry would march 2nd Platoon to their extraction zone while Lieutenant Kim's patrol rejoined the 66th. And Cassius? Well, he would be free to begin another assignment. There was no shortage of mortals to save and demons to hunt. *Or, God willing, my atonement will be complete, and my place in Heaven restored.*

'Will the wildlife ever come back?' Hudson asked. Witnessing the jungle bereft of life was an odd experience. Except for the crunching of boots, the only sounds came from leaves rustling in the breeze and water trickling in the streams.

'Evil's spell is fleeting. Life will return. It always does,' Cassius answered.

Hudson subjected the big marine to a sideways glance. 'You're not how I imagined an angel to be,' he stated tentatively.

Cassius raised an eyebrow. 'And how should an angel be, Randy Hudson?'

'I don't know,' Hudson admitted. 'Not so badass, at any rate.'

Cassius smiled. 'I told you before, Randy. I'm a soldier like you.'

Private Hudson shook his head. 'Angels and demons,' he muttered in disbelief. Despite the horror, Hudson found himself reassured by events. Knowing there was something more, something beyond death, was a comfort, especially when he'd lost so many friends and not least poor Larry. The existence of angels, even if they did transpire to be considerably more violent than he was led to believe, was a genuinely uplifting revelation.

At the target site, the soldiers were met by a pungent black smoke swirling into the predawn sky. A great swath of the jungle had been obliterated by napalm, the evil corrupting the land purged by fire. Around the pit, hundreds of dead soldiers and toppled trees littered the scorched ground.

Stepping through a carpet of thick ash, Cassius crossed to the edge of the foul-smelling nest and peered into the darkness below. 'Heavens above, that's rife,' he muttered, grimacing. 'It's enough to bring tears to the eyes.' Stretching out his hands, the yawning black abyss was instantly brightened with white light. Deep inside lay the reeking remains of a giant creature, its smouldering body charred black, its stunted wings bent and broken. *Barbequed demon. Nice.*

Turning from the pit, Cassius allowed the light to fade. 'The monster was close to completing its transformation. The wings were all but formed. It appears we stopped the beast just in time.'

'It's dead then?' Lieutenant Perry questioned, eager to press north. He couldn't wait to leave this godforsaken nightmare behind him.

Cassius nodded. 'I'm glad you found your courage, Richard. You and your men fought bravely. May you navigate this war to its conclusion unscathed.'

The survivors of Death Valley prepared to part company. An exchange of handshakes and respectful bows took place beside the pit. Private Hudson bade a final farewell to the man… no, the angel who had saved them all from Hell.

'Will I see you again?' he asked.

'I don't think so, Randy. Not unless you find yourself embroiled in another demonic plot.'

Hudson looked disappointed. 'That's a shame. My mom would love to meet a real angel.'

Cassius smiled. 'Well, who knows. Perhaps I'll pop by once in a while. If you notice a stranger at church giving you a nod and a wink, you'll know it's me.'

Randy grinned, but while shaking hands, he saw a figure emerge from the bombsite over the angel's shoulder. Ash-blackened and smouldering from head to toe, the man staggered through the choking fumes as if his next step would be his last.

Oh my God, how has he survived? Hudson mused, horrified by the man's terrible injuries. His head lolled as if his neck was broken, and his limbs didn't move like they should. Despite the man's charred features, the private recognised him. 'Sergeant Powell?' Hudson said, edging closer.

Hearing his name, the man's head twitched upright, and to Hudson's dismay, his dead eyes shone red through the billowing smoke.

'Keep away, Randy,' Cassius warned.

Staff Sergeant Powell emitted a low, almost animal-like moan. Then, with speed beyond the capabilities of any cripple Hudson had ever seen, he leapt at the private like a pouncing tiger, grasping for his throat with skeletal fingers.

Hudson fell into the sea of ash. He tried to scramble away, but the red-eyed zombie grabbed a flailing leg. Having snared its prey, the undead began dragging Hudson back into the choking black haze from whence it came.

Staff Sergeant Powell didn't get far. A flaring light brightened the gloom, and the red-eyed soldier was incinerated into human dust. 'Holy Mother of God!' Springing to his feet, Hudson rubbed the vaporised remains of his sergeant from his eyes.

The meaning behind this latest zombie attack was not lost on Cassius. *I knew it was too easy*, he mused grimly. And now, that dreadful meaning was confirmed beyond any doubt. A disturbance northwest of the blasted landscape revealed the awful truth of his darkest nightmares, and Cassius' nightmares were dark. The tall trees swayed back and forth as if buffeted by a mighty storm. Then, preceded by a terrible bestial cry, a vast winged shadow rose into the sky, soaring above the jungle.

'Volgamare,' Cassius hissed through gritted teeth. 'Our victory is snatched from our grasp!'

The soldiers stared in terror as the enormous creature circled high above, its shrieking call as horrifying as its ungodly appearance.

'A dragon,' Hudson whispered in dread. 'A black dragon.' Never had he witnessed anything so disturbing. Despite the warmth of the jungle, fear climbed his spine like an icy winter chill, freezing his heart. 'There were two all along.'

'Yes, Randy. And now our task will tax us to our limits. The creature's minions will come for you as before. You'll need to stand firm until I return.'

'Where are you going?' Hudson asked despairingly. How could they hope to survive another onslaught without the angel to protect them?

Cassius pointed skywards. 'I must confront the demon,' he said solemnly. 'Defeat the volgamare, defeat its minions.'

Under the incredulous gaze of the soldiers, Cassius blazed with light. Consumed by flame, the big marine was gone. Cassius stood before them adorned in the white and gold armour worn by Heaven's battle angels. Launching into the air, he tore through the smoke-cloaked sky like a rocket.

Below, appearing from the grey and black smog, advanced the enemy, a second army of the dead.

'Fall back to the pit!' Lieutenant Perry cried.

Hoping to use the enormous hole to their advantage, the soldiers assembled on the far side of the smouldering demon nest. They would gain valuable time if they could force the enemy around the obstacle. *Time enough, God willing, for the angel to slay the dragon*, Lieutenant Perry prayed.

Angel and demon met above the battlefield. Cassius struck the volgamare like a raging fireball, smashing against the beast in an explosion of searing white-hot flame. Stunned by the impact, the winged monstrosity plummeted from the sky, wheeling end over end as it fell toward its doom. Yet before crashing into the jungle, the demon regained its senses, and its great leathery wings lifted it high once more.

Cassius leapt onto the creature's back, blasting its scaly black hide with angel light until it blistered and bubbled beneath his gleaming hands. Shrieking in agony, the volgamare rolled over and over, desperately trying to dislodge its unwanted passenger. But the angel held on. Twisting its huge horned head, the monster belched its acrid breath at its foe, a lethal gas capable of stripping flesh from bone. Cassius hurled himself aside, but in doing so, he left himself vulnerable to the beast's swinging tail which slammed into him like a colossal sledgehammer. Knocked unconscious by the savage blow, the angel was sent streaking earthward like a flaming meteorite.

Private Hudson saw Cassius disappear amidst the trees to the north. 'Lord have mercy, who will save us now?' He watched in dread as the volgamare swooped low to join its army. 'Take Cover!'

The beating of the beast's wings heralded the unleashing of its toxic breath. The acid struck the centre of Lieutenant Kim's line, and his men fell screaming into the pit, their skin stripped from their bodies.

'We won't survive another attack like that,' Lieutenant Perry stated gravely. And to compound their misery, the undead had almost worked their way around the sides of the pit. 'Save your ammo until you can see the glare of their red eyes,' he ordered.

Meanwhile, halfway up a very tall tree, Sergeant Griffin closed his eyes. 'Don't look down,' he told himself. He had never been much of a climber. Not even when he was a kid. 'One branch at a time.' He felt terribly exposed, especially from the winged devil in the sky. 'Almost there, just a little higher.' He just hoped it was going to be high enough.

Arrow-straight and miraculously unscathed by napalm and dragon's breath, the lone teak stood amongst the debris like a symbol of hope. It was almost as if the tree had been spared for a reason. At least, that's what Sergeant Griffin thought. It was a sign from above.

Realising what needed to be done, Griffin had bolted for the tree just as the creature's minions closed ranks, ensnaring his brothers-in-arms. A split second longer and the undead would have trapped him too. 'Fortune favours the brave,' he muttered wryly. Wedged between the teak's highest branches, Sergeant Griffin unslung his radio. 'This is 1ST Battalion, 7TH Cavalry, B Company. Broken Arrow! I repeat, Broken Arrow!'

'Open fire!' Lieutenant Perry ordered. The remnants of 2nd Platoon and their NVA allies squeezed their triggers, releasing a deluge of screaming lead smashing into the enemy's unholy ranks. The zombies dropped in their droves, but as before, they soon clambered to their festering feet to recommence their march. Armed with Ak-47s, the undead soldiers of the NVA's 66th Regiment closed for the kill.

Once the soldiers' ally, the great pit had become their doom, and with nowhere to go, the undead pressed them ever closer to the nest's gaping mouth.

Sergeant Griffin was in trouble too. He'd been found. The enemy gathered around the teak, intent on dislodging the radio operator from his lofty perch. Shots were fired, but fortunately for Sergeant Griffin, being dead evidently hindered his would-be assassins' aim. A trio of zombies attempted to ascend the tree, but much like their marksmanship, climbing was proving to be another problematic skill to master beyond the grave.

'What the hell is Griffin doing?' Lieutenant Perry muttered. He'd spotted the sergeant nestled at the top of the only tree still standing within a five-hundred-yard radius. Then Perry understood. He also understood the precariousness of the sergeant's situation.

'We need to protect Sergeant Griffin,' Lieutenant Perry yelled. Their lives depended on his survival. It was all or nothing. This was the lieutenant's moment to lead from the front. This was his moment of destiny. 'Attack!'

Lieutenant Perry charged at the undead's centre, and with his M16 hammering, he scythed a path straight through their ranks. He'd never felt such elation, and to his genuine surprise, his men were right behind him.

Lieutenant Kim slashed with his machete, Private Hudson stabbed with his bayonet, and Corporal Lamar, having rearmed with AK-47s, blasted the red-eyed monsters into pieces with a machine gun grasped in both hands. The last of the living hit the zombies beneath Sergeant Griffin's teak tree like an avalanche, blasting the undying with everything they had left.

'Secure the tree!' Lieutenant Perry bellowed, raking an enemy soldier with lead. Now that the angel was gone, Griffin was their only hope. He alone could coordinate the air strike.

Private Hicks cried out in pain. A bullet had shattered his left femur, and in an instant, the stricken soldier was hauled away by the undead hordes and torn to shreds.

Hudson riddled an uncommonly tall NVA officer with so many holes he could see the rising sun shining through his torso. A zombie blasted Lieutenant Kim with its AK-47, the bullets mangling his left arm. Taking the hit, the North Vietnamese officer swung his machete with his right arm, hacking the undead soldier's head from its shoulders.

Capturing the tree, the men pressed their backs against the bark and prepared to make their final stand.

The army of the dead encircled them, a horde of crimson-eyed abominations. Above, a gigantic black shadow approached, eclipsing the smog-veiled sun. Swooping low, the volgamare began its final run.

The soldiers defending realised it was over. They lowered their guns to the ground, defeated. Amongst the branches of the teak tree, Sergeant Griffin stared aghast as the giant winged creature dropped from the sky toward him. The thing's enormous maw, lined with vicious black teeth, opened wide, ready to unleash its terrible breath.

A bright flash blinded Griffin. Then, straight after, a wave of heat crashed into him, buffeting him as if he were caught in the heart of a raging storm. He clung to the branches, fighting to hold on. A thunderous roaring filled the skies. As the sergeant's vision cleared, he saw two jet fighters screeching through the air and the monster wreathed in flame.

The F-4 Phantom's sidewinders blasted the volgamare off course but swiftly did the demon recover. Shrieking with fury, it soared high in pursuit of the US fighters. As the creature climbed into the sky, the path was clear for a second aerial assault. Booming through the valley, ground-attack aircraft roared into view. Sergeant Griffin directed their approach, and soon A-1 Skyraiders and A-4 Skyhawks dropped their payloads onto the enemy. Huge eruptions of flame detonated amidst the undead's ranks, hurling their bodies into the air.

Above the destruction on the ground, the volgamare beat its leathery wings hard and fast, propelling its immense frame straight at the fast-approaching warplanes. The Phantoms had circled for another attack, and now, head-to-head, machine and monster hurtled toward one another. Having spent their missiles, the pilots opened up with the aircraft's rotary cannons, hammering the demon with 20mm shells at a hundred rounds per second. The bullets bounced screaming from the beast's toughened hide, neither harming nor dissuading it from its collision course.

With afterburners howling, the fighter jets pulled hard into the vertical, but the monster's deadly breath spewed into the sky, shrouding them within a hissing cloud of toxicity. The airframes melted around the horrified pilots, the acid-like gas eating through the metal at a ravenous rate until, igniting the fuel tanks, the jets exploded into a pair of screaming fireballs.

On the ground, private Hudson covered his eyes from the blast. 'Now we need a miracle,' he whispered.

Having unleashed their bombs, the ground-attack aircraft were already on their way home, leaving Hudson and the last survivors to face their fate alone. The undead regrouped, and the winged demon wheeled high above them, manoeuvring itself into position once more.

Hudson gripped his crucifix, praying for salvation. He stared at the new day rising, believing it would be his last. But then, out of the corner of his eye, he noticed a shining white light climbing into the sky above the distant trees. 'I'll be damned.'

Cassius ascended through smoke and smog, soaring higher and higher until bathed in the sun's magnificence. Presenting himself before the burning star, he absorbed its pulsing rays until every fibre of his being burst with light. No living creature was designed to hold such power, and Cassius risked annihilation. Yet he was a warrior sent from Heaven, battle-hardened by countless centuries of war. He was a guardian angel, a demon hunter, and seldom had he encountered a monster he could not defeat.

The volgamare began its dive, plunging through the gloom to destroy its victims, a vast winged shadow of doom.

'Don't try this at home, ladies and gentlemen,' Cassius muttered wryly. Using himself as a conduit, he unleashed the sun's limitless power at his foe, a supercharged beam of pure angel light. 'Roast in Hell!' The unerring pulse of energy struck the demon with the destructive force of a nuclear warhead. A colossal inferno of erupting flame and searing heat exploded across the sky, and when the air cleared, both angel and demon were gone.

Surrounded by the fallen dead, the survivors stared into the crimson sky.

'Do you think Cassius is dead, too?' Hudson whispered. 'Can angels even die?'

Corporal Lamar shook his head. 'Nothing could have survived that,' he said soberly.

Grim-faced, Hudson surveyed the battlefield. 'We deserve medals for what we did here.'

Lieutenant Perry gazed at the dead North Vietnamese soldiers heaped at his feet. 'We'll get medals, alright,' he replied. 'But for all the wrong reasons. No one will believe what happened.'

The men heard the distant hum of helicopters, a distinctive thumping growing louder and louder. The 7th Cavalry had come to take them home.

'Can someone help me down from this tree!' Sergeant Griffin yelled.

~ The End ~

Demon Hunters

Zen Lee & The Yellow Emperor

In Ancient China, a young woman will make a stand against evil, and her courage will herald the dawn of a new order: The League of Demon Hunters.

But before the League, there was the Brethren.

Demon Hunters

Heroic Fantasy through the Ages

Demon Hunters

The Black Knight

~ A Tale of Sir Lancelot ~

Dark-Age evil rises. The realm is in peril.
Witchcraft & sorcery plague the land.
The queen is missing. The king is at war.
Hope is a knight in black.

Camelot's greatest champion must return to save Arthur's kingdom.

Demon Hunters

Heroic Fantasy through the Ages

Timothy Williams: Book One
Demon Hunter

When Timothy's school becomes the subject of a demon takeover, he and his two friends, Rupert and George, must unmask their foe. Timothy is forced into a battle for survival, not only in the real world but in his very dreams, where he must fight his nemesis to prevent Hell on Earth.

'A full-on teenage adventure. Original, humorous, and highly imaginative. A rip-roaring read!'

Blood-thirsty battles, monstrous demons, dodgy haircuts, and enough possessed wildlife to fill a satanic zoo!

Timothy Williams: Book Two

The Infernal Shadow

Timothy, Rupert, and George return for their second year at Great Underwood Upper. Yet, with Lucifer back with a vengeance and Ursula Le Rouge more determined than ever before, it promises to be Timothy's most hellish challenge to date.

Hell on Earth?

Not if Timothy can help it.

'A bit like Buffy the Vampire Slayer but with English accents, possessed squirrels and apocalyptic land wars from the mists of time!'

Coming soon…

Timothy Williams: Book Three
Hellfire & Angel Light

The Chronicles of Cassius: Volume Two

Skuzz Buckets: Series One

ABOUT THE AUTHOR

Iestyn Long lives with his family in the historic village of Lavenham, in the Suffolk countryside. He is reasonably tall and narrow but desperately running out of hair, and although English, he has a Welsh name that is a constant confusion to one and all. While listening to the tunes of Sir Cliff, Iestyn enjoys observing ants, stroking sparrows, drinking copious amounts of tea, and breathing. Iestyn writes fantasy fiction for teen freaks and grown-up geeks. Expect high-adventure, monstrous demons, dark humour and epic battles.

For loads of extra demon-hunting stuff, visit the website:
https://www.demon-hunter.co.uk

www.ingramcontent.com/pod-product-compliance
Lightning Source LLC
Chambersburg PA
CBHW020330030826
48979CB00021B/508